"The little ones
are so fragile,
aren't they?"

DOUBLECROSS

MISSION HINDENBURG

THE 39 CLUES

C. ALEXANDER LONDON

WITHDRAWN

SCHOLASTIC INC.

To Ben and Dillon and all the
adventures they have ahead

Library of Congress Control Number: 2015936087

ISBN 978-0-545-76746-0

10 9 8 7 6 5 4 3 2 1   15 16 17 18 19

Library printing, August 2015

Printed in the U.S.A. 23

Scholastic US: 557 Broadway • New York, NY 10012
Scholastic Canada: 604 King Street West • Toronto, ON M5V 1E1
Scholastic New Zealand Limited: Private Bag 94407 • Greenmount, Manukau 2141
Scholastic UK Ltd.: Euston House • 24 Eversholt Street • London NW1 1DB

CHAPTER 1

Palm Beach, Florida

The seasonal citizens of Palm Beach, Florida, shuffled beneath the neatly tended palm trees along the sidewalk, rushing to catch their dinner reservations. The Outcast checked his watch.

4:45 P.M.

Oh, how he loathed the average member of his generation! For the wealthy retirees who wintered in Palm Beach there was little to do but shop at the luxury stores along Worth Avenue, lunch at the Beach Club, then dine out at five before settling into the evening's police procedural shows on television.

The Outcast locked his sleek gray Lexus and strolled beneath the Spanish-style colonnade that welcomed visitors to a—Cheesecake Factory?

He grunted. Chain restaurants. To his right and to his left, nothing but chain restaurants.

What an ignoble place, he thought, *for a Cahill to die.*

When he reached the gate he was looking for, he straightened his tie and pressed the buzzer.

A long time passed until finally a sharp voice blurted through the speaker, "Who is it? I'm just sitting down to dinner."

"Beatrice," the Outcast said. "I've brought you a gift."

He reached into his pocket, pulled out the small porcelain figurine he'd purchased for just this occasion, and held it up to the security camera. The statue was about the size of his palm, a smiling red-cheeked cat wearing small white wings, its paws extended as if in flight. A ghastly piece of "art," but it was sure to do the job. Beatrice loved her porcelain cat figurine collection.

A moment passed, and then the gate swung open. He strolled inside to a quiet courtyard where a sad cluster of potted plants had begun to wither. Beatrice had, no doubt, neglected to care for them herself and was too cheap to hire a gardener.

She opened the door at the rear of the courtyard and stood in front of him with her hands on her hips and her painted-on eyebrows raised in surprise. Her lips bore the ghastly shade of hot pink that she had been wearing for decades, smeared clownlike over her too-thin lips.

"I don't like unexpected guests," Beatrice told him.

The Outcast smiled. "You recognize me after all these years?"

She nodded slowly without moving to invite him in. "I didn't at first. But now that I see you in person, I know exactly who you are. A psychic once told me that I am an excellent judge of character. Always have been, ever since I was a little girl. Faces change but a man's character never does."

"And are you glad to see me?" the Outcast asked her.

"You shouldn't be here," Beatrice snapped. "Not after what you've done."

"Then you want me to go?" He raised an eyebrow.

Beatrice acted as if she were studying her long false fingernails against the doorframe. Her voice rose to a mouselike pitch. "I didn't say *that*. You've come all this way . . . and you say you've brought a gift?"

The Outcast couldn't help but smile. *No, character never changes.* He held up the winged cat figurine. "Why don't we have a cup of coffee and catch up? I'd love to hear all the juicy gossip since I've been away."

Beatrice pointed at herself. "Gossip? Me? I never gossip. . . ."

The Outcast waited.

"But it *has* been an eventful time." She whistled. "Oh, the stories I have, you wouldn't believe. You know I raised Grace's two grandchildren and you're surely aware of what ungrateful teens they've become. Oh, don't just stand there, come in and I'll tell you all about it."

The Outcast nodded.

"But first, let's have that Cupid cat," Beatrice said, greed lighting her eyes. "It'll go perfectly in my collection."

"It isn't Cupid," the Outcast told her as he crossed the threshold into her condominium. "It's Icarus." He cleared his throat, feeling ridiculous even saying it. "Cat Icarus."

"Icarus," Beatrice repeated. She obviously had no idea what that meant.

Beatrice had gone to the finest schools, but she had the intellectual curiosity of a three-toed sloth.

He lifted the winged cat figure up. "From Greek mythology."

"Oh, of course," Beatrice said. "Obviously." The corner of her mouth twitched.

"You know the story," the Outcast said. "How Icarus and his inventor father, Daedalus, were imprisoned inside the Minotaur's maze on the Greek island of Crete. To escape, Daedalus built two pairs of wings out of feathers and wax so he and his son could fly from the island together. He warned his prideful young son not to fly too high, for if he got too close to the sun, its heat would melt the wax that held the wings together. The boy, filled with the arrogance of youth, flew as high as he could on his borrowed wings. As he'd been warned, the wax melted, and the boy plummeted to his death in the sea."

"Well," Beatrice muttered with a shake of her head. "I prefer less gruesome stories, but of course it is a nice lesson for young people, I suppose, to respect their elders."

"Indeed," the Outcast agreed. He handed her the figurine. "Careful not to drop the little fellow. He'd shatter into a million pieces."

"The little ones are so fragile, aren't they?" Beatrice said as she placed the statue carefully into her winter collection of cat figurines. There were at least fifty of them staring down from the shelves, farmer cats and doctor cats and spy cats and even a custom-made Beatrice cat, complete with hot pink lipstick. "I'll go get that coffee," Beatrice said with her back to him as she studied her cat collection proudly. "I only have instant. I hope you don't mind."

"Actually, Beatrice, I won't be staying long enough for coffee," the Outcast said. He pulled a syringe from his pocket as Beatrice turned to face him. Her jaw went slack, her eyes bulged.

"Now, there's no need for that . . ." she croaked out. "And anyway . . . I'll—I'll scream."

"No one will hear you," he said calmly. "It's dinnertime in Palm Beach and you can be certain all the televisions are cranked up very, very loud. You should have chosen somewhere else to winter."

He rushed for Beatrice, who swung to block him. Her long nails raked across his cheek, but he caught her wrist and spun her around with one hand, gripping her tightly against his body. She squirmed but could not break free.

The Outcast pressed the syringe into her neck as he whispered in her ear, "You shouldn't have recognized me, Beatrice. It would have been so much better for you if you hadn't."

CHAPTER 2

Beverly Hills, Los Angeles, California

"Yo, I *know* that the first RoboGangsta movie broke a billion-dollar box office, which is *why* now's the time to make *my* movie!" Jonah Wizard shouted over the phone. "I've told you a hundred times! It's about a kid from the streets who just wants to be a mime!"

He paced through his swank living room, gesturing wildly. Giant black-and-white photographs of Jonah gazed down from the walls of the room, and sunlight streamed in from the floor-to-ceiling windows that looked over his infinity pool. Beyond it, Los Angeles shimmered in the heat of midday.

The sky over Los Angeles was turning gold and red with the sunset. The palm trees that ran along the city streets cast long shadows, and streaks of soft pink light painted the stark white walls of the Wizard crib with delicate stripes.

As Jonah argued with his father/business manager, Amy, Dan, Hamilton, Ian, and Cara sat on the white leather sofa, staring at the deep-pile black rug on the floor. It seemed to change color the longer you stared at it, blue-black to black-blue to black-black to off-black.

Amy hadn't even known off-black was a color.

"I *do too* know about the streets! Daaad!" Jonah's voice grew shriller than Amy Cahill had ever heard it. The sound pierced through her exhaustion, through her worry, and made her want to toss her teenage superstar cousin's phone out the window . . . but she couldn't interrupt him. The money he made off his Hollywood career was the only money they had, now that an old man calling himself the Outcast had staged a coup to take over the Cahill family and cut off all of their access to the Cahill bank accounts, even the secret ones.

Amy had been all too happy to hand over the reins of the Cahill family to Ian Kabra, who had been all too happy to take over leadership of the most power-ful family in the world. He'd said it was the role he was born to play.

He didn't get to play it for long.

The Outcast had kicked Ian out of Cahill head-quarters in Massachusetts, turned most of the branches of the family against Ian and his friends, and vowed to re-create four famous disasters from history that the kids would have to stop, if they could. They'd already foiled his attempt to sink a re-creation of the *Titanic*. One down, three to go.

Now all they could do was wait.

Waiting was not something Amy enjoyed.

"Would you please get off that infernal phone

call!" Ian Kabra finally blurted. Apparently, waiting around was not something he enjoyed, either.

"No!" Jonah yelled. "No way!"

Ian's face flushed. Amy tensed. When Grace Cahill, Amy's grandmother, had been in charge of the family, she would never have allowed her authority to be so openly defied. She'd cast people out for less, even her own husband. And Amy knew for certain that Ian's parents had killed people for less. Amy wondered what Ian might do.

But Jonah kept yelling. "I will *not* add a werewolf to the story, Dad, no matter how much the fandom wants to see it!" Jonah ended the call. He hadn't been yelling at Ian at all—he'd been yelling at his father.

Amy relaxed.

"Sorry about that, Kabra." Jonah shrugged. "Show business, you know?"

"I most certainly do *not* know," Ian replied.

"Jonah, you sure you want to make a movie about a mime?" Hamilton Holt asked his cousin. He was Jonah's best friend, cousin, and bodyguard, and right now he looked genuinely worried about Jonah's career choices.

Jonah shrugged. "It's a drama about the silencing of the artist in the noise of contemporary pop culture."

"Uh . . ." said Hamilton.

"And RoboGangsta wasn't my thing," added Jonah.

"But I *like* RoboGangsta," Hamilton told him. "Stuff blows up."

"If you would both *please*!" Ian Kabra interrupted them. "Might we not discuss the relative merits of *stuff blowing up?* We have only just averted a disaster of 'titanic' proportions and we don't yet know what the Outcast has in store next."

Just then Amy's phone buzzed in her hands. She frowned down at it.

"It's Aunt Beatrice."

Aunt Beatrice was their grandmother Grace's sister, but what Grace had had in charm, daring, and intelligence, Beatrice had in greed, gossip, and cheapness. She used her slice of the Cahill cash to spend half the year in Florida, as far from Amy and Dan as she could get without having to learn a foreign language. She spent the other half in Boston, disapproving of them.

"What's *she* want?" Dan asked.

"She sent us a text," Amy told him, more puzzled than ever.

"That doesn't sound like her," said Dan. "She doesn't even know *how* to text."

Amy held up the phone so Dan could see.

The text contained only two words:

Look up

"I don't think that is from your Aunt Beatrice," Ian said as he looked up through the wall of glass, past Jonah's infinity pool, to a blimp that had settled itself in the air over Los Angeles, framed perfectly in the center of Jonah's windows, a public air show aimed at just the six of them.

CHAPTER 3

They rushed to the windows and looked at the blimp, which hovered in place, silhouetted against the darkening sky. The red glow around the edges of its black shadow looked like a bullet wound in the sky.

"Maybe we should get away from the windows," Hamilton suggested, thinking of bullet wounds and snipers.

"I don't believe our enemies would send a dirigible to neutralize us," said Ian.

"Neutralize," Cara scoffed. "That's a Brit-fuff-fuff way of saying you don't think they're trying to kill us. But you know, Kabra, they are."

Ian clenched his jaw. As leader, he needed to keep his emotions in check and not get riled up. However, no one could rile him up quite like Cara Pierce. She seemed to derive some kind of twisted pleasure from needling him at every turn.

He smiled at her.

Ian had once heard a $500-per-hour guru tell his father that the simple act of smiling, even a false smile, could alter one's mood. By smiling, he hoped his mood would be altered from frustrated confusion to calm, cool, and collected confidence, as befitting a Lucian of his standing.

Cara met his smile with one of her own.

How she infuriated him! Her smile was so much better than his!

"Amy." Ian turned away from Cara, stiffening his back. Something was afoot, and it was his job as leader to do something about it, not to get distracted by Cara. "Does the text message say anything else? Anything about a dirigible?"

"Stop saying *dirigible*," Cara snapped at him. "Just call it a blimp like a normal person."

Ian frowned at her. He preferred the word *dirigible*, and it meant the same thing.

"No, nothing about a blimp," said Amy. "Just 'Look up.'"

"Well, perhaps you should call back, then," Ian suggested.

As Amy moved to press CALL, an LED panel below the blimp's gondola lit up with bright red letters scrolling in a loop over and over again. Dan read the words aloud:

"'According to Brueghel
when Icarus fell
it was spring

a farmer was ploughing
his field
the whole pageantry

of the year was
awake tingling
near

the edge of the sea
concerned
with itself

sweating in the sun
that melted
the wings' wax

unsignificantly
off the coast
there was

a splash quite unnoticed
this was
Icarus drowning'

"A message from the Outcast?" Dan wondered.

"That's a poem, bro," Jonah told them all. " 'Landscape with the Fall of Icarus,' by William Carlos Williams. He was a great twentieth-century American poet."

"You memorize poetry?" Dan wondered.

"How do you think I became the best hip-hop lyricist of our time?" Jonah said. "Tupac read Shakespeare. He was a Janus. When I was starting out, I studied all the poetry I could. So I know my boy W. C. Williams wrote this poem."

"I never had much fondness for the American poets," Ian replied, dismissing Jonah's boast. "Does the poem tell us anything useful?"

Jonah shrugged. "It's a poem about a painting by the sixteenth-century Flemish artist Pieter Brueghel, *Landscape with the Fall of Icarus*. Well, it's a copy of Brueghel's painting style. No one knows who actually made it. There's a lot of debate in art circles about the actual painter of this particular work of—"

"Jonah!" Ian snapped. "We don't need an art history lesson."

"Right," said Jonah. "So, the painting in question shows a ship sailing out of a harbor and a farmer plowing in his fields. Everyone in the painting is looking in the wrong direction while Icarus drowns in the Aegean Sea. Only his tiny legs are painted in the corner, see?"

He tapped a panel on the wall and one of his pictures turned into an image of *Landscape with the Fall of Icarus*. Every photo in the room was actually an LED screen. The high-resolution picture of the painting was so clear you could even see the brushstrokes on the canvas. Ian tapped the screen where Icarus's legs kicked helplessly at the sky, ignored by the farmer who kept plowing his field.

"So this is about looking in the wrong direction?" Ian suggested. "This message is a hint that *we* are looking in the wrong direction. Could your Aunt Beatrice be trying to warn us?"

"Beatrice wouldn't know that," said Dan. "And

probably wouldn't warn us if she did. Anyway, where would she have gotten a blimp?"

Ian pursed his lips. He would have preferred suggestions rather than just criticism of his idea. This had to be the start of the Outcast's next threat. "What do you think, Amy?" he asked.

She shook her head. "I guess I can call her back."

"Speakerphone," Ian snapped a little too forcefully. If Ian was going to prove to the others that he was the right leader for the Cahills, he couldn't always be letting Amy figure things out. He had to be the one managing this situation.

Amy put the call on SPEAKER.

The phone rang.

And rang.

And rang.

And then a voice answered, a man's voice, one Ian recognized from the day he was tossed from the mansion in Attleboro and lost control of the family. The Outcast.

"Hello, children, good of you to call," the Outcast said. "I trust you've read the poem."

"Where is Aunt Beatrice?" Amy snapped at him.

He didn't answer.

Ian took over the conversation. "Why have you sent us this poem?"

"Consider it your next clue," the Outcast said, chuckling to himself. "The next disaster I have planned for you."

"We stopped you once, we shall do it again," said Ian. "Perhaps you would stop wasting our time and tell us why you're really doing this. If you wanted to undermine my leadership, there are simpler ways."

"Oh, Ian Kabra," the Outcast said. "How like a Lucian you are, assuming it is *your* time to waste. It is *my* time. I decide how you spend it and how much of it you have. And if you want to prevent a terrible loss of humanity, I suggest you get busy before history repeats itself. He who flies closest to the sun will surely fall burning to the earth. Good-bye now, children—"

"Wait!" Amy pleaded. "Please, where is Aunt Beatrice?"

The Outcast laughed again. He seemed in a merry mood, which annoyed Ian even more. Amy's hands shook.

"You care so much about that old cow?" the Outcast asked.

"She's family," Amy said.

"If only everyone shared your sentimentality, Amy Cahill," the Outcast told her. "Unfortunately, your Aunt Beatrice didn't make it."

Amy swallowed hard and Ian saw her face tighten even as the rest of her body seemed to slump. "The coroner will call it natural causes," the Outcast continued. "And I suppose he's right. She was naturally a gossip and it caught up with her at last. Now, get to work, children. As they say, time flies. And so must you. The Karman Line will be crossed."

With that, the call went dead. Amy stood still as a statue as Los Angeles darkened in the window behind her. The streetlights and the lights of houses flickered on, like a carpet of stars, while the smog above made the sky smooth and blank. Behind Amy, the blimp still floated between the false stars on the ground and the blank sky above, scrolling its poem. Slowly, it turned and began to float away.

"Yo, I don't want to alarm anybody, but William Carlos Williams was from New Jersey," said Jonah.

The others looked at him blankly.

"Why should we be alarmed about New Jersey?" Ian wondered, but Jonah didn't answer him. Amy did.

"The *Hindenburg*," said Amy gravely.

"The what?" Dan replied.

Amy seemed to snap out of a trance as she spoke. "I thought there was something odd about what the Outcast said. He told us there would be 'a terrible loss of humanity.' Why say it that way? Why say *humanity*?" She tapped a search into her phone and then held it up so everyone else could see what she'd found.

In black and white, they saw the frame of a giant zeppelin burning, people in a field, running away. The large balloon that held the passenger gondola below shimmered and flickered with flames, tilting to the ground at an impossible angle as it suddenly sank to the earth, smashing apart. The skin of the balloon melted away and the frame collapsed in a heap of burning fabric and scorched metal.

Jonah hit another button and the black-and-white disaster footage replaced the Icarus painting on the large screen on his wall.

Tiny figures in fancy clothes ran from the wreckage of the crashing zeppelin in panic and dismay. Rescuers rushed toward the flames in futile acts of heroism, and the crackly voice of an old-time radio reporter cried out, his voice choked with tears, "This is the worst disaster . . . Oh . . . oh, the humanity!"

Amy turned her phone back to herself and read: " 'On May 6, 1937, the passenger zeppelin *Hindenburg* burst into flames while attempting to dock in Lakehurst, New Jersey. Thirty-six people were killed.' "

" 'Time flies and so must you.' " Dan repeated the Outcast's words as all eyes turned to the blimp floating away over downtown Los Angeles.

"We have to follow that blimp!" said Ian.

CHAPTER 4

"I'm cracking the flight data," said Cara, flipping open her laptop and typing at the speed of light. "If they're floating over downtown LA, you can be sure they had to file a flight plan. We can see where they took off and where they're supposed to land."

Ian stood over her shoulder, watching her type, while the others stared out the window at the blimp making its way across their view of the Los Angeles sky.

"Shouldn't we call someone?" Ham asked. "If the Outcast is going to re-create the crash of the *Hindenburg* and there's a blimp floating over LA right now, couldn't that be the one he's going to blow up?"

"We can't simply call the authorities without proof," Ian told him. "The police might think that *we* are the ones making bomb threats. And, if you'll recall, I am not a United States citizen. Your Homeland Security agents are suspicious chaps."

No one could argue with that logic, so they let Cara continue to work with Ian breathing over her shoulder.

Amy and Dan stood side by side at the window.

After a long silence, punctuated only by the clicking

of Cara's keyboard and her occasional grunts and mutterings, Dan spoke. "The Outcast killed Aunt Beatrice."

Amy nodded. Beatrice hadn't ever been kind to them, or generous or loving or any of the things one would want a guardian to be, but still, she'd always been around, and now she wasn't. She was dead. Amy wasn't actually sure how she felt about that.

"Beatrice didn't even want to be involved in the Cahill family," Dan added. "It's our fault she's dead, isn't it?"

Amy turned to her little brother and saw the serious look etched across his face. However confused she felt about Beatrice, she didn't feel at all confused about her brother. "It is not our fault," she told him firmly. "We didn't want to be involved, either, remember? It's the Outcast. It's *his* fault. Don't forget that. Don't forget that for a second."

Dan studied her. "You're right. I won't forget it again."

"You believe me, don't you?" Amy looked him in the eye. He was still shorter than she was, but barely. He was growing, and fast. He was quickly becoming her not-so-little brother.

"I believe you," said Dan, setting his jaw. "We've got to stop him. He's a murderer."

"We're going to stop him," said Amy.

Dan glanced over his shoulder. "You think Ian's up to it?" he whispered. "Leading this family like Grace did?"

Amy shook her head. "No one could lead this family like Grace did. She was . . . special. But I think Ian can do it, if we help him."

She hoped it sounded convincing.

"I got it!" Cara cried out. "The blimp is owned by a company called Daedalus Entertainment— and before you ask, *Ian*, yes, it's a shell company and *no*, I can't find anything else out about it. The blimp took off from a private hangar only five miles away! And it's scheduled to land there again in half an hour."

"We need to get there right away," said Ian. "The *Hindenburg* exploded when it was docking after a flight. If that's what he has planned, we don't have much time. We'll take two of Jonah's vehicles."

Jonah had only gotten his driver's license a year ago, but he'd already filled an eight-car garage with luxury vehicles.

"Ham," Ian instructed. "You will drive Dan, Amy, and Jonah in the armored BMW. Cara and I will take the Aston Martin Q series."

"Oh, we will?" Cara raised her eyebrows at him.

Ian immediately blushed. "Well, I mean, I thought you could, perhaps, well, tell me more about this, you see, the . . . eh . . . shell company while we . . . er . . . drove?" he stammered.

Cara patted him on the back. "Don't get all flustered, Kabra. I'll go with you in the Aston Martin. But I'm driving. No offense, but I don't trust you to drive on the right side of the road."

"I know how to drive an automobile!" Ian said back to her, his blush turned to red anger.

"Yo, Kabra, why do you get to take my Aston Martin Q?" Jonah asked him. "That's the sweetest ride I own. There are only five of them in North America."

Ian narrowed his eyes. "Leadership is a grave responsibility," he told Jonah. "Therefore it comes with commensurate privileges." He looked at his watch and then at the group. "Now, let's go stop a disaster!"

CHAPTER 5

The black BMW peeled out in front of them, and Cara jolted the sleek silver Aston Martin Q from the garage in its wake, careening around the marble fountain in front of Jonah's mansion. She sped through the front gate, and the engine purred like a wildcat.

"I texted you the GPS coordinates of the hangar," Cara said over the speakerphone.

"Take the shortest route," Ian added from the passenger seat. Cara gave him a side-eye look, which he did not believe he deserved. He was simply being thorough. He'd found, when managing Hamilton Holt, it was best to be specific.

"You know I trained in evasive driving when I became Jonah's bodyguard, right?" Ham told them over the speakerphone from the car in front.

"I am aware," Ian replied.

"So try to keep up," Ham snapped back, and then the BMW took a sudden sharp left, and Cara had to slam the brakes and spin the wheel not to miss it. They broke the speed limit immediately, hitting 65 miles per hour on a quiet street through the hills. Hamilton wove into the opposite lane to pass slower-moving cars, and Cara followed. Ian tried not to clutch the armrest too tightly. He wanted to impress Cara with his calm in the face of danger and his faith in her driving, but in his chest his heart thumped so loud it was a wonder she couldn't hear it.

Hamilton turned left and then a quick right and another left, avoiding the rush hour traffic on Sunset Boulevard.

"Don't lose him," Ian told Cara.

"Roger that, Captain Obvious," she replied.

He decided to keep his mouth shut. In truth, he was relieved she'd insisted on taking the wheel. Ian always did forget which side of the road Americans drove on.

At the next turn, Cara slammed on the brakes, barely stopping in time to avoid smashing into the back of Ham's car. In front of them a wall of red brake lights blocked their path.

"LA traffic," Ham said over the speakerphone.

Ian checked his watch again. He glanced up at the sky but couldn't see the blimp overhead. "There is simply no way we can make it to that hangar in the next fifteen minutes," he said. "It's not possible."

"I got Jonah from the premier of *RoboGangsta* to an after-party in Pasadena in less than twenty," Ham said.

Ian had no idea if or why that was supposed to impress him, but it didn't matter right now. All that mattered was getting to that hangar.

"Cara, you ready to do some real driving?" Ham asked.

Cara revved the engine in response. She ran her hands along the leather-covered steering wheel.

"Yo, don't break my ride," Jonah piped in, and then the BMW took off, turning hard toward the parking lot of a large glass building. Cara followed him. They wove between parked cars, then stayed right behind Ham's car, knifing down an alley and onto a sidewalk, and then took a hard left into oncoming traffic.

Brakes squealed and cars honked, but Ham's car accelerated.

Cara pressed the gas. "No guts, no glory!" she said, speeding over the top of a hill and turning into a parking garage after Ham. They raced up one side of the parking garage, down another, and burst onto the neighboring street where she had to do a jack-knife turn to spin the car 180 degrees in place, then shoot like a bullet down another hill, which took them under an overpass. Ham sliced his car from side to side, passing a bus by pulling halfway onto the sidewalk, then reversing when he hit traffic on a crossing avenue to take a different route the wrong way down a one-way street. He turned into a narrow alley, which threw sparks off the doors of Jonah's car as it scraped through.

Ian could hear Jonah groan over the speakerphone.

Cara kept up, her hands gripping the wheel at ten and two o'clock. Her eyes scanned the traffic, the streets, the sidewalks, and kept Ham's car in sight. *What a remarkable person*, Ian thought. She was mesmerizing and unbelievable, able to hack a government database and drive in a high-speed pursuit through Los Angeles. He felt fairly useless in the passenger seat, like he was cutting in on a dance between Cara and the car. He had to assert himself if she was to remember him at all.

"Watch out for that rubbish bin," he said, as she swerved around a trash can.

Foolish! He had to offer her more than that! As he formulated something else of value to say to her, it took him by complete surprise when she hit the brakes. His body slammed against the seat belt and then jolted him back into his seat, whiplashing his neck in the process.

"Why are you stopping?" he cried out, looking at his watch in a panic.

"Because we're here," Cara pointed out.

Ian looked up and saw they had stopped at the perimeter fence outside a large hangar with a parking lot and a concrete landing pad in front of it. The fence was topped with barbed wire and only had one gate all the way on the opposite side.

The blimp itself hovered over the concrete, slowly lowering over the landing pad. Its giant silver balloon rippled in a light breeze, and dust kicked up from its landing rotors, which stabilized the descent.

"It's coming in now," Ian gasped, popping out of the car. He turned back quickly to Cara. "Lovely driving, by the way."

She narrowed her eyes at him and he regretted immediately that he'd said anything. He meant it as a compliment, but it had, of course, come off as sarcasm.

No time to explain, though. It was time for action. He slammed the car door and turned to to Ham. "Can you get us through this fence?"

Hamilton gave a quick nod, bent at the knees, and gripped the metal wire with his bare hands. He grunted and heaved, and the wire gave, bending just enough from the ground for them to slip underneath.

The airship dropped six lines and a ground crew ran out to hold them, to help bring in the blimp. If it exploded now, they would surely all be killed. Ian knew he had to save them. It was up to him, lives in the balance, and he had no time to dillydally.

"Jonah," Ian barked. "You stay here with the cars. I don't want anyone recognizing you. Everyone else, come with me."

Ian sprinted ahead toward the landing pad, hoping the others would follow. This, he felt, was leadership, running first into danger, come what may. Still, he glanced over his shoulder to double check that they were, indeed, behind him.

The ground crew was so busy bringing in the flying machine that they didn't notice Ian and the other kids running toward them until they were in shouting distance.

"Back away!" Ian warned them. "She's going to explode!"

But by the time they heard him, the blimp had touched down, its engines whirring to a stop, and the crew stood face-to-face with Ian as he caught his breath.

"How did you get in here?" one of the men demanded.

"We have . . . to get the pilot . . . off the blimp . . ." Ian panted. "It's going to blow!"

"There is no pilot," the crewman told him. "It's remote controlled. We were hired just to fly it around for an hour. . . ." He pointed to the gondola on the ground beneath the rippling silver oval above. "Who are you kids?"

Ian ignored him and rushed forward to look inside the cockpit.

The crewman was right, there was no pilot. The cockpit was just a control board with gears and levers and transmitters linked to a computer terminal for the remote pilot on the ground to control the blimp. But Ian went pale when he saw what was attached to the control board.

There was another bright LED screen with a picture of a bright blue sky and puffy white clouds rolling by. In front of the clouds, a clock counted down. Wires led from the clock to a row of neatly bundled bright white plastic explosives.

"Bomb!" he shouted.

Amy, Dan, and Ham turned to run, waving their arms for the crewmen to back off. "Bomb!" they repeated. "Bomb!"

The crewmen ran.

Cara, however, paused. She pulled out her phone and snapped a photograph, just as Ian dove at her, wrapping his arms around her waist and hauling her onto his shoulders.

"What are you—?" she objected, but he ran with her as fast as he could, making it about twenty yards before there was a flash of light, followed by the roar of the blimp exploding behind him.

CHAPTER 6

Dan had tasted plenty of dirt in his life, from his elementary school days getting picked on by bigger kids to the countless falls, chases, and explosions he'd survived during the Clue hunt and its aftermath. If he had to pick, though, he'd say that the Los Angeles dirt was the worst tasting, and now he had a mouth full of it. He spat out the gravel and scraggly brown grass that he'd taken full in the face and sat up.

Amy was beside him, rubbing her head. The others were spread around the parking lot, where they'd taken cover or been knocked down, slowly getting to their feet. Cara was tangled with Ian for some reason, and Ham had two crewmen pinned beneath his massive arms, where he'd probably thrown them for protection from the blast. He was like that, always putting himself between danger and other people.

Right in front of Dan, the blimp burned on the landing pad. The explosion had ripped the gondola to shreds, and there were sizzling shards of metal scattered all the way to the hangar. Orange flames danced and crackled where the cockpit had once been. The gas had burned off fast and left a thick black cloud rising into the heavy Los Angeles sky. It probably wouldn't make much difference with all the pollution already in the air, Dan figured, but still, the smell was pretty bad.

"Are you okay?" Amy asked him.

He nodded. He'd ducked and covered in time. The confused crewmen staggered to their feet. Cara untangled herself from Ian, and Ham helped them both up. Jonah ran from the cars to join them, waving his arms in the air. Dan noticed that Jonah was running away from a heap of burning wreckage behind him, on the other side of the fence.

"Shrapnel!" the teenage superstar cried out. "Burning shrapnel crushed my Aston Martin."

Dan recognized now that that burning heap beside the fence was Jonah's once luxurious limited edition silver Aston Martin Q. The $350,000 sports car had been reduced to a smoking heap of scrap metal.

Jonah shook his head sadly. "She was a beauty . . . but yo, when that blimp blew, the sky lit up like day. I thought you guys were goners."

"Yet it seems no one was hurt," Ian announced proudly. "Apparently, we have thwarted the Outcast's intended disaster rather effectively. Some *Hindenburg*! That explosion had no more import than a minor crash at one of those air shows you Americans are so fond of."

Something nagged at Dan. It didn't feel right. This was hardly a disaster. Even if the bomb had gone off without the kids' warning, the six guys on the ground might not have been injured, and there was no one on board the blimp to get killed. And unlike when the *Hindenburg* crashed in 1937, there were no cameras to film it so that kids a hundred years later could watch it on the Internet like they had back at Jonah's. There had been worse airship disasters before the *Hindenburg*, disasters that had killed more people. What made the *Hindenburg* disaster unique was that it had been filmed. It only took thirty-two seconds to burn up, but the whole world could watch those thirty-two terrible seconds over and over again.

This lonely little blimp explosion didn't seem like the *Hindenburg* disaster at all.

This seemed like a diversion. Like the painting of the fall of Icarus . . . everyone looking the wrong way while the real disaster happened.

"I don't think this was the Outcast's disaster," Dan said.

"Certainly it was," said Ian. "He led us right here."

"But I don't think he's done yet." Dan turned to his sister. "You said the *Hindenburg* was a zeppelin, right?"

"I did," said Amy.

"Well" — Dan pointed at the burning mound of fabric and metal — "*that* was a blimp."

"What is your assertion, Dan?" Ian scoffed. He turned to the flaming blimp and opened his arms wide at its wreckage. "That was the blimp on which the Outcast detonated an incendiary device."

Dan wrinkled his forehead.

"A bomb," Cara clarified. "Kabra, speak English."

"I am!" Ian blurted in exasperation. "That blimp blew up because the Outcast put a bomb on it. It burned on the landing pad just like the *Hindenburg*."

"Except it didn't," Dan argued. "Because a blimp and a zeppelin aren't the same thing."

"Of course they are," said Ian. "It's like how I say 'take the lift' when you say 'take the elevator.' The words are different, but the object they refer to is the same."

"No, they're not," said Dan. "They're both airships, also called dirigibles — which is really just fun to say — but *blimps* keep their shape from the pressure inside their inflatable envelopes, kinda like giant helium balloons. They don't have rigid hulls. Really, a blimp is just a big gasbag." He paused and looked Ian up and down. "You know what that's like, Kabra."

Amy elbowed him in the ribs. It was worth it, though, to see Ian's nostrils flare.

"Anyway, *zeppelins* have rigid hulls," Dan continued. "Frames with flexible fabric stretched over them so they keep their shape whether they're full of helium, hydrogen, or any other gas. No matter how much the pressure changes, a zeppelin looks like a zeppelin. That's why the video we saw online was so dramatic. The *Hindenburg* kept its shape when the hydrogen inside lit up, all the way until . . ." He made an explosion noise.

"How do you know so much about airships?" Ham wondered.

Dan shrugged. Amy wasn't the only one who was allowed to know stuff.

"Thirty-six people died when the *Hindenburg* exploded," Amy said, which made Dan feel bad about his sound effects.

She had a way of reminding him that history wasn't just crazy stories but was stuff that happened to real people, stuff that real people did or didn't do. Usually, stuff that some old Cahill did or didn't do.

"The *Hindenburg* was one of the first disasters ever caught on film," Amy said. "It was the first time people actually saw the moment of destruction and death for themselves, instead of just hearing it described. It also ended the era of airship travel. Everyone had thought zeppelins were the future. They were going to be the most luxurious and efficient way of getting around ever imagined. There were even plans to have airships dock on the needle at the top of the Empire State Building in New York City. When the *Hindenburg* burned, it ended an entire industry."

"See?" said Dan. "So this explosion was nothing like that one. There was nothing fancy about that blimp."

"I agree. Something about this isn't right. The Outcast wouldn't think so small," Amy said. "If he was going to re-create the *Hindenburg* for real, he'd want something that people were watching. Something that could horrify the world and ruin a brand-new industry."

"Like space travel?" Hamilton Holt suggested.

"Yes," said Amy. "That would do it."

Ham pointed.

A billboard had been posted along the entire side wall of the hangar. It showed an image of the sky with an airship drifting across it—a futuristic zeppelin rising into space. The text of the ad said:

THE AIRSHIP X PRIZE
ATHENS, GREECE

AN AIRSHIP RACE
FOR THE
EDGE OF SPACE

"'He who flies closest to the sun will surely fall burning to the earth,'" Dan said, repeating the Outcast's words aloud.

"The edge of space seems pretty close to the sun," said Ham.

"The Outcast did say the Karman Line would be crossed," said Dan.

"What on earth *is* the Karman Line?" Ian wondered.

"The Karman Line's not on Earth," Dan told him. "The Karman Line is an imaginary line sixty-two miles above sea level that marks the edge of space. It was named after the Hungarian physicist Theodore von Kármán."

Amy raised an eyebrow at him.

"What?" he said. "Space is cool."

"I think it's time we get out of here," suggested Ian. "We'll all have to squeeze into the BMW. Jonah, I highly recommend you report your Aston Martin stolen before the police show up at your so-called *crib* with inconvenient questions. And then we'll need to book your private plane."

No one questioned Ian's leadership this time, and they all ran together for the car, the one that wasn't a smoldering heap of burning junk in the parking lot.

Jonah and Ham looked at the ruined roadster.

"This is why we can't have nice things." Ham sighed. "Guess I can't borrow it for my date next week, huh?"

Jonah shook his head sadly. "I don't think your boyfriend would be impressed by a heap of burnt metal."

Dan and the others all turned to look at Ham and Jonah in surprise.

"His *boyfriend*?" Dan wondered.

"Oh, right," said Jonah. "I figured you all knew."

Ham stared at his feet, suddenly blushing.

"I guess we do now," Dan told him. "Cool."

Ham looked up again. Smiled.

"When this is all over, maybe we'll get to meet the lucky guy?" Amy suggested.

Ham nodded, laughing.

"I hate to interrupt this touching moment of acceptance and camaraderie," Ian said. "But we are trying to prevent a killer from re-creating one of the most terrifying aerial disasters of the twentieth century. Hamilton's dating life is hardly more pressing than that."

Ham nodded with a look of relief that the subject had been changed, and he opened the heavily armored BMW door for the others to get in. When he settled into the driver's seat, Ian ordered him to "step on it."

They had to get to Athens, and fast. According to the billboard, the airship race to the edge of space was scheduled to start in Athens, Greece, the very next day.

"You know," Dan pointed out. "The fall of Icarus took place in Greece, too."

CHAPTER 7

As they drove back to Jonah's, Ian sat wedged between Amy and Cara. Jonah had insisted on taking the front passenger seat, or "shotgun" as the Americans called it, with as much dignity as could be expected from citizens of a country where one could order a breakfast called the Rooty Tooty Fresh and Fruity. Dan had his head resting against the window opposite, staring up at the sky, and Amy seemed content to watch her brother.

Ian felt a pang as he thought of his own sister, how they could comfort each other in their own ways when they suffered a tragedy. It had usually involved shopping or mocking the incompetent help at middle-class hotels, but still, it was the special comfort of family that he missed. He was glad that Amy still had her brother. He felt sometimes like a brother to her as well, like an older brother, responsible and wiser. He wished she saw him that way, too. He did so want to prove himself a worthy leader to Amy Cahill.

He shook the thought away. What should it matter what she thought? He was in charge, as he was meant to be, and *that* was all that mattered.

He turned to Cara, who was staring down at her phone. He felt a pang when he looked at her, too. Was this the pain of leadership? He wanted so badly to keep everyone safe. Especially her. He'd never tell her that, though. She'd kick him in the shins before she'd let him think *he* could protect *her*.

Still, he had to try.

"Why didn't you run when you saw the bomb?" he asked her quietly. The lights of Los Angeles flickered on her face as they drove.

"Because I needed to get this picture," she said. She held up her phone. It was a photo of the bomb, slightly blurry because Ian had been tackling her as she took it. "I'm running it through AnarchiNet, a dark image database online."

"Well, naturally," Ian said, although he had no idea what that meant.

"AnarchiNet is on the deep web. Not just anyone can access it or search it, but I know some people . . ." She let the thought trail off. She had a dark side, Cara Pierce did, and oddly, Ian found that side of her compelling as well.

"I'm confirming what I suspected," she told him. "This bomb type is one favored by KGB agents decades ago. It's been used in Russian mafia bombings as well."

"Alek Spasky, Irina's brother, was a KGB assassin," Ian said. "And we know he's in league with the Outcast."

Ian looked over Cara's shoulder out the rear window. The traffic on the side streets they were taking back to Jonah's wasn't so bad. A few cars changed lanes behind them. One turned on to the street, another turned off. Nothing suspicious. Ham was being very careful to obey the speed limit.

Still, if Alek Spasky was following them, it would be hard to tell. The man was an expert at espionage and murder, and Hamilton Holt was a teenager who had taken a three-day defensive driving course.

"Hamilton," Ian called to the front seat. "Do you know how to lose a tail?"

"Of course," said Ham. "I have to ditch Jonah's paparazzi all the time."

"Then I suggest you take precautions now," Ian suggested. "To be on the safe side."

Without a moment's hesitation, Hamilton jerked the wheel, slamming the brakes into a spin and accelerating out of the spin again so they were moving in the opposite direction in the opposite lane. Anyone who was following them would have to do the same in order not to lose them.

No one followed and Ian let out a sigh of relief. He was not eager to come across Alek Spasky again. The last time, the assassin had nearly killed them all.

As they pulled up to Jonah's house, Amy turned to Ian. "Before we go to Athens, I want to know if anyone else thinks it's strange that the Outcast did all that just to get us to look at a billboard."

Ian had thought the same thing. "He's not just trying to re-create disasters," he said. "He's trying to keep us busy."

"Too busy to find out who he is, maybe?" Amy suggested.

Ian was impressed. Amy was a quick thinker. He wondered how she felt, turning over the leadership role to him. He wondered if he could have done the same if he were in Amy's shoes.

Of course, he would never be caught dead in Amy's cheap shoes. He wore handcrafted leather wingtips.

"If the Outcast was someone Grace expelled from the family, someone who had knowledge of KGB sleeper agents like Alek Spasky, there's probably a connection to Moscow," Cara added. "And any Cahill-KGB connection would've had Lucian fingerprints all over it. If there are clues to who he really is, I bet they're in the Lucian stronghold in Moscow."

Ian smiled. Leave it to Cara to consider the devious connections. She had the kind of calculating mind he'd need if he was ever to bring all the branches of the family back under his unified leadership again.

"I'll call Nellie," Amy said, dialing already.

"Hey, kiddo!" Nellie Gomez's voice filled the back of the car. "We're just through customs at LAX and we're heading to Jonah's place now."

"Sorry, Nellie," Amy said. "I need you two to turn around. We're off to Athens and you've got to get the next flight to Moscow. We think there will be files there that can lead us to the Outcast—a KGB connection to anyone Grace expelled from the family."

"Got it," said Nellie without hesitation, solid as ever.

Ian smirked to himself, admiring Nellie's unquestioning obedience, but his smile froze when he looked back down at his phone.

He had typed in a search for the Airship X Prize and he'd brought up a news article about the competition. He hadn't read a word yet, but with one flick of his thumb scrolled down to a photo list of all the different corporate sponsors of the competing airships. The third one down sent a chill through him. There was a large silver airship shaped more like a submarine than a balloon. It was in some sort of high-tech hangar, and a group of executives and engineers posed proudly in front of it. And in that group, staring up at Ian, was a man who had pledged his loyalty to the Outcast and had laughed as Ian was tossed from the Cahill mansion. He wore a gray pin-striped suit that Ian would have recognized anywhere. It was custom-made for him from rare Italian silk and had been a gift to the man on his fortieth birthday from his children . . . Ian and Natalie Kabra.

Ian was looking at a photo of his father.

If a murderous plan was underway, he could be sure Vikram Kabra was a part of it.

Attleboro, Massachusetts

Saladin, that nightmare of a cat, hissed from inside his crate. The Outcast noticed that he hadn't touched the cans of cat food he'd had left out while he was in Florida.

"Grace spoiled you," the Outcast told the cat. "You will get no red snapper from me."

He smirked, then punched a button on his remote control. A portrait of a seventeenth-century duke over the fireplace slid to the side to reveal a 46-inch flat panel screen. The screens were one of the many technological advances the kids had installed when they had the estate rebuilt. He found himself rather glad to be inheriting the mansion after them.

The pale face and steel blue eyes of Alek Spasky filled the screen.

"So they followed the clues?" the Outcast asked him.

"Exactly as you wanted them to," he said. "I lost them, however, as they were leaving the airfield. Would you like me to reacquire them in Athens?" Spasky asked.

"There is no need," the Outcast said. "I have plenty of agents in place to keep them occupied. I need you to go to Moscow."

"Moscow?" Alek pursed his lips. "I haven't been home in years."

"I think you'll enjoy this visit," the Outcast told him. "You once told me you held Amy and Dan responsible for the death of your sister, Irina."

"I do," Alek responded.

"Well, you will get your chance to take from them someone they care for," the Outcast told him. "Nellie Gomez and the Mourad boy are snooping into my business and I would like them stopped."

"Killing two birds with one stone," Alek said with a joyless grin.

"Three, actually," the Outcast added. "It's not enough merely to stop the two of them. I believe it's time to take care of that entire viper's nest lurking below the Kremlin."

The smile that broke across Alek's face this time looked positively gleeful.

The Outcast shut off the screen and let the portrait slide back over it. While Amy and Dan Cahill and their friends scurried around the world to prevent a great and tragic fall, they wouldn't notice as he rose higher than they could ever have imagined.

CHAPTER 9

Somewhere over the Atlantic

Jonah's private jet ran into turbulence over the Atlantic. Ian muttered curses as he tried to get the spilled soda out of his pants, while Cara tried to stifle her laughter at his lunatic hopping around.

Amy reviewed what they had uncovered about the Airship X Prize. It was a prize meant to stimulate the private spaceflight industry. Over the last decade there had been competitions for civilian teams to launch satellites, to invent new kinds of rockets and communication systems, and to create the possibility for colonization on Mars through high-speed engines and even recycling human waste into potable water.

"Astronauts drink their own pee," Dan observed.

"Well, it's filtered, distilled, and sterilized," said Amy. "This prize has invented all kinds of technologies and encouraged billions in new aerospace spending."

"Billions at stake?" said Dan. "That sounds more like a Lucian plot."

Ian had showed them the picture of his father, and Cara's quick searching online had turned up Omnia

Industries, a Lucian-owned investment company, as one of the airship sponsors. They were pretty sure that if a Lucian airship was there, none of the other competitors were safe. Lucians weren't known for their sense of fair play, and Ian's father was one of the worst of the bunch. He was also openly loyal to the Outcast. Now they knew they were headed in the right direction.

"So this competition is for the highest subspace orbit of a passenger airship," Amy said, reading from one of the articles. "The teams are all trying to launch airships that can cross the Karman Line."

"I still don't get why anyone would want to," Ham said.

"It'd be awesome if one of these airships could pull off getting there," Dan told him, his face lighting up. "See, it's easy to launch into subspace, but it's not easy to go fast enough to stay there. It takes huge amounts of energy to reach the speed of eight kilometers per second that you need to orbit the earth. Gravity in subspace is almost as strong as gravity on the surface of the earth, so in order to orbit, you have to basically fall sideways around the curve of the world faster than it's spinning. To get that kind of speed takes all kinds of fuels and booster engines and heat shields . . . but an airship uses gas mixtures, right? So if someone could invent one that just kind of *drifts* into orbit from the ground, it would make spaceflight safer and cheaper than anyone ever imagined. You wouldn't need such crazy speed to stay up, and by flying at the edge of space you could cover huge distances fast. In subspace orbit it only takes about an hour and a half to go around the world, so it would take just a few minutes to fly to Europe. You could go to China for lunch, Australia for a jog, and be back home for dinner."

Dan took a breath. The others stared open-mouthed at him.

"I didn't know you were into space travel," Amy said.

Dan shrugged like it was no big deal.

Amy marveled at her brother. He wasn't reading this from anywhere. She'd seen his photographic memory at work countless times but never seen him geek out on something like space before. Geeking out was usually *her* thing.

"It *is* amazing," Amy agreed. "Air travel causes huge carbon emissions, a major contributor to global warming. These airships could almost totally eliminate the carbon footprint of air travel. Just think about it. How much carbon do the Cahills alone pump into the atmosphere? We practically live on airplanes."

"If you don't like it, you can get out and walk," Jonah joked. A bump of turbulence wiped the grin off his face almost instantly.

"There'd be almost no turbulence on an airship." Cara grinned at Ian. "You'd never spill soda on your fancy pants again."

"I do *not* wear 'fancy pants,'" said Ian. "I wear sensible slacks that fit properly, and I will not apologize for taking pride in my appearance."

"Wow, defensive," Cara said. "I meant it as a compliment. I *like* your fancy pants."

"Oh, well . . ." Ian blushed. "Then thank you."

"So, guys, not to interrupt this *fascinating* conversation about Ian's pants," Dan piped in, "but there are six airships in this competition and we don't know which one is going to go all *Hindenburg* and explode."

"What'd the Outcast say?" Cara wondered. " 'He who flies closest to the sun will surely fall burning to the earth'?"

Dan nodded. "And 'the Karman Line will be crossed.' "

"Has an airship ever risen that high before?" Amy asked.

Dan shook his head no.

"Then that must be it, right?" Cara asserted. "Whichever ship gets to that line sixty-two miles up is the one he's going to target. The one that flies closest to the sun."

"But how would the Outcast know which ship that will be?" Amy wondered.

Ian leaned forward and tapped the article on his phone screen. "With my father and the Lucian leadership involved, you can be sure it won't be left to chance. They'll have chosen the target and rigged the competition."

"So," said Amy, who understood what Ian was suggesting about his father's plan. "We're not looking for the airship that's been sabotaged."

Ian nodded. "We're looking for the only one that hasn't."

Athens, Greece

Jonah's plane taxied to a stop on a private airstrip in the early morning. Mist shrouded the hangar and cast the limo idling by the runway in a ghostly silhouette. The suited men standing around the limo gave Ian pause.

"Relax, yo." Jonah patted Ian on the shoulder. "Those are just the local security guys the studio hires to keep the paparazzi away."

"How would the paparazzi even know you were here?" Dan wondered. "*We* didn't even know we'd be here ten hours ago."

"They always know where Jonah is," said Hamilton. "They're better than any spy agency in the world. That's why I, as his bodyguard, have to be better than they are."

"Right on!" Jonah gave Ham a fist bump, and they both opened their hands and made explosion sounds.

"It is perhaps in very bad taste for you two to 'blow it up' right now," Ian said.

"Ian's right," said Cara, which made Ian's chest

swell a bit. She had her laptop open and was looking at the Airship X Prize page. "We've got to stay focused on the problem here. Today all six airships are doing a demonstration flight. None of them will try for the Karman Line until tomorrow, so this is our chance to figure out which of the six ships he's targeting."

"Five," corrected Ian. "If Omnia Industries is behind one of them, then we know that one won't be the target. My father made it very clear whose side he was on when he joined the Outcast. You can bet he's running this plot from that ship, which leaves us twenty-four hours and *five* potential targets."

"You're thinking we should split up?" Amy asked him.

"It is the most efficient use of our time," said Ian. "While you investigate each of the airships to determine which they will allow to go the highest, I will board the Lucian airship to see what I can find out from my father's people."

"I'm not sure splitting up is the best idea," Amy argued. "Someone is going to end up on board a flying bomb and you'll be going into enemy territory alone."

Ian bit the inside of his cheek. Why must Amy question him all the time?

"I am in charge now!" he yelled. "It's my turn! Why can't you just follow orders? Why must you peck at me all the time? Peck, peck, peck!"

"Kabra, chill." Jonah tried to calm him.

Cara just stared at him and Amy looked at the floor, obviously embarrassed, but not for herself. She had the nerve now to pity him for making a spectacle of himself.

But he couldn't stop.

"I have made my decision!" He sat back down, crossing his arms. "Anyway, a Lucian airship is not 'enemy territory.' I am their rightful leader and they are my family. I know how to handle them better than anyone here ever could! Ever!"

"My only question, *sir*," Amy added in mock formality, "is how do we even get on these airships? There's a huge prize at stake. They're not going to just let some kids stroll on board. And, family or not, the Lucians will certainly know you're not supposed to be there, Ian."

Ian clenched his jaw. Trying to give Amy Cahill an order was like trying to flap his arms and fly: exhausting and ineffective.

She'd never blindly follow his leadership, and the others continued to look to her for guidance. Now he'd made it obvious he couldn't control her. He would have to try a different strategy to get Amy to do as he wished, something he found rather loathsome: He'd have to explain himself.

"One person is easier to hide than five or six," Ian explained. "And we do not have time for all of us to inspect each ship together. There is less danger of being discovered. There is a chance our presence will force the Outcast to detonate his target early. If we split up and one of them does explode while we are still investigating—"

"Not all of us will die," Dan finished Ian's thought. A grim silence fell over the cabin of the plane. Ian had to say something to break the mood of foreboding.

"I believe every one of you is capable of inspecting an airship safely on your own. I have absolute confidence in you."

He stared at Amy and she stared back at him. Splitting up really was the only option he could think of. It wasn't ideal, but she was not offering a better solution.

All eyes looked from Ian to Amy.

"That still doesn't answer how we'll actually board each of these ships," Amy said.

All eyes went back to Ian.

"Well . . ." Ian explained. "That is where we'll need Jonah's assistance."

"I can get myself on board the airship sponsored by Galactica Toys," Jonah said. "They're the European distributor for the RoboGangsta action figures and baby kitchen sets."

"Perfect," said Ian. "So you'll board that ship and assess its chances of winning, but first we'll need to use some of that Wizard magic to get the others on board their respective airships."

"You want me to cause a distraction?" Jonah asked.

"As only a celebrity of your inexplicable renown can do," said Ian.

"You know, sometimes I feel like the only contribution you want from me is my fame," Jonah said. "Like, I've got more to offer than just making my fans riot."

"Yes, yes, of course you do, Jonah," Ian dismissed him. "Perhaps you can hold a press conference to tell everyone all about your new artistic endeavors in *RoboGangsta 2*."

"Yo, Kabra, I told you I'm making *Silent Song* next," Jonah said. "The one about the mime."

"Wonderful. Your fans will be dying to hear about it," said Ian. "And while they are enraptured by Jonah's discussion of his place in the history of cinema and the under-appreciated art of mime, we will use the distraction to slip on board our respective airships. After the demonstration, we'll coordinate our findings to establish which airship will be the Outcast's most likely target at the Karman Line."

"And then what?" Amy asked.

Ian clenched his jaw so tight a rigid line of muscle swelled along the side of his face. "And then we will figure out how to stop it from exploding!" he said. "This is my plan. I don't hear another one, so if you don't mind, we've got an aerial disaster of historic proportions to prevent."

Everyone waited for Amy to give a slight nod, as if her approval was needed, even Cara. It felt like an ice pick had stabbed Ian in the back, but he kept his face locked in what he hoped was a confident expression. Leadership was not nearly as pleasurable as he had imagined it would be. He had assumed that as leader, his commands would be followed without question or delay. He had never expected so much . . . doubt. He wished the others would look to him the way they looked to Amy or even better, the way they had looked to Grace. She was someone who did not abide doubt.

"Let's get to it," he snapped.

Jonah made a phone call back to LA so that he could arrange his press conference, and Cara and Amy looked over the descriptions for each of the experimental airships, while Dan fidgeted and looked up at the sky. Ian could swear the boy had a smile forming on his lips.

Ian felt far from smiling. As they stepped from the plane and piled into the limousine, he quietly feared he had just ordered at least one of them to step on board a flying bomb. If things went wrong, the death of one of his only friends would be on his hands. *This is how a general must feel before a battle.*

Why, he wondered, *would anyone want to be a general?*

The weight of his last name hung around his neck.

Would he really be able to outfox his father, the criminal who had disowned him, disgraced him, and joined a coup against him, the man who had taught Ian everything he knew about ruthlessness?

He also wondered: If it came down to it, would his father really let him fall from the edge of space, as Daedalus let his son, Icarus, fall into the sea?

CHAPTER 11

Moscow, Russia

"Try to blend into the crowd," Nellie Gomez suggested to Sammy Mourad as they strolled among the tourists outside the candy-colored spires of the Kremlin. Bright redbrick walls ringed the massive square, and the cool autumn sunshine glinted off the gold Byzantine domes that capped the roofs of the famous towers. Green-clad ceremonial guards marched in formation through the plaza as camera flashes clicked.

"I don't think I'm the one who needs to worry about blending in," Sammy replied as he lifted Nellie's hoodie up to cover the bright streaks in her hair.

"Let me take a picture of you," she told him. "It will make us look like we belong."

She lifted her phone up and Sammy struck a touristy pose, trying to smile. Nellie tapped the focus on her camera to the background. She wanted to assess the situation at the entrance to the Lucian stronghold beneath the Kremlin. The only way in was through the State Kremlin Palace, a monolithic theater of glass and white marble constructed during the

Soviet era. While the grand and colorful towers of the Kremlin's famous buildings were built by the tsars in order to showcase their wealth and taste, the State Kremlin Palace was erected by the Soviet Union, the empire that came after them, in order to showcase its power.

People had lined up outside it for guided tours, and police stood by the main doors to keep anyone unauthorized outside.

"You know how to get inside?" Sammy seemed doubtful of the whole course of their investigation.

"Amy and Dan snuck into the Lucian base here during the Clue hunt," she explained. "We'll get in the same way they did."

"And what do we do then?"

"We dig into the secret files to see what we can find out about an Outcast with KGB connections," she told him.

"Remember what Beatrice said to us before she went to Florida?" Sammy asked. "That Grace made a lot of her enemies into outcasts . . . even her own husband. She said Grace had him assassinated, right here in Moscow."

"That was just a vicious rumor," said Nellie.

"But what if it *is* true?" said Sammy.

"Look," Nellie said at last. "We're not here to investigate Grace Cahill's past. We're here to investigate the Outcast's. What Grace did or didn't do has nothing to do with it."

"I hope you're right," said Sammy.

Nellie guided Sammy through the crowd, beneath the spires and domes of the Kremlin, and they joined a line of tourists waiting to enter the State Kremlin Palace. The building loomed over them, the glass catching the sunlight and glistening like ice. Tall as it was, most of the structure was actually underground. Inside there was a world-class theater where world-class acts performed.

Tonight's show was the Tohashi Hibachi Brothers, a trio of Japanese brothers who cooked elaborate meals on stage, juggling shrimp and sushi, tossing knives and spices, to the ooohs and aaahs of the crowd. Nellie had always wanted to see them, but she knew this would not be her chance. With any luck, she and Sammy would slip inside, find what they were after, and be on a plane to meet the kiddos in Athens by evening.

She checked her watch. The tour wouldn't take them in for another ten minutes. Once they were inside, they'd leave the group and sneak into the Lucian base through Balcony Box 4, Row 3. She'd typed the trick to open the door into her phone so she wouldn't forget it.

Suddenly, Sammy pulled her from the group.

"We have to go," he whispered as he tugged her away.

"What? Why?" Nellie freed her arm.

"Turn here." Sammy pulled her to the left, away from the ticket booth. "We're being watched."

Nellie glanced around her hoodie and the hair on her neck prickled at what she saw. There was a man trailing them through the crowd. He wore a loose-fitting wool overcoat and wool watch cap pulled over his head, but his face was clear. His cold blue eyes locked with hers. Then she saw a small steel rod drop from his sleeve and begin twirling around his finger, faster and faster, a blur of metal.

Alek Spasky, ex-KGB assassin, Irina Spasky's brother, and the Outcast's merciless button man, had warned them that the next time he saw them, they'd get one of his steel rods in the back.

When Nellie's eyes met his again, he winked.

And the steel rod flew from his fingertips.

Nellie dove, knocking Sammy to the ground. The rod whizzed past them and sparked off a marble column, leaving a gash in the grand monument to Soviet architecture. Nellie popped up to her feet and pulled Sammy back up to his.

"Vandal!" Nellie shouted, pointing at the damaged pillar and at the man with the steel rod, another of which was already twirling on his finger. She hoped the word *vandal* sounded enough like the Russian word for *vandal* to get the attention of the surrounding tourists.

Almost immediately, people began to call out for the police. The crowd swarmed the mysterious man, shouting at him. He began to knock them off, weaving and chasing after Nellie and Sammy through the crowd, but he was overwhelmed by angry Muscovites grabbing at his sleeves. The police began to make their way over.

"I guess he did us a favor," said Nellie as Alek's face disappeared into the swarming crowd.

"If you call trying to kill us a favor," Sammy replied.

"No," said Nellie. "But look."

She pointed to the door into the building. The guards were distracted by the commotion out front, and the police were busy trying to peel angry citizens off the vandal. Nellie and Sammy slipped inside the building that housed the Lucian stronghold without anyone noticing.

They raced through the lobby and followed the signs for the balcony. As they ran, Nellie pulled out her phone and found the place she'd noted with the code. The theater walls were all blond wood, the seats a deep blue. It wasn't like one of the grand theaters of Europe or even Broadway in New York City. It was huge and severe and unsettling, built to awe the audience as much as provide a venue for performances.

"There's an order we have to sit in these seats," she told Sammy. "45231. Do it!"

Sammy sat in seat 4, then seat 5, then 2, then 3, then 1. There was a small clicking sound behind the curtain at the far end of the box. Nellie rushed over and pushed open a secret panel door. They slipped through and pulled it shut behind them.

They were inside the Lucian stronghold, one of the network of secret bases that the different branches of the family had built all over the world. From this base, the Lucian family had launched revolutions and counterrevolutions, run vast spy networks, controlled shadow industries, and laundered ill-gotten fortunes of immeasurable value.

Nellie and Sammy were definitely not supposed to be here.

They raced down a narrow corridor. Floor lights, like in the aisles of an airplane, guided them to a bank of elevators. Nellie had notes for the elevator code in her phone, too. She felt almost as if she were chasing Dan and Amy's past as she entered in the proper numbers and the elevator door slid open. They whooshed down deeper into the Lucian stronghold. Sammy chewed his lip nervously as they descended. Nellie pointed at the elevator wall behind them.

"The kiddos told me they saw a giant portrait of the Kabra family on that wall when they snuck in here," she said. "I guess the Lucians took it down."

Sammy nodded. Nellie didn't like how quiet he'd gotten. He must be terrified. She wasn't exactly comfy herself, but she could've used some small talk to lighten the mood. Instead, she listened to the rumble of the descending elevator until they came to a stop and the doors opened onto another long hallway.

They both froze as two Lucians in lab coats disappeared around a far corner, lost in their own conversation.

When the coast was clear, Nellie checked her phone and led Sammy to another door, which opened into a large room covered with full-size portraits of famous Lucians from the past. Doors ringed the room, and she wasn't sure which one to take.

Amy and Dan had gone to an office when they were here, but she was after some sort of archive or file storage. She walked the perimeter of the room, looking at the portraits. The nearest portrait was of Napoleon. When Nellie pushed open the door beside his portrait, she saw a long corridor lined with gun safes and yet more steel doors locked with digital keypads. So the portrait of Napoleon led to the armory, she guessed.

She moved to the door beside the portrait of Sir Isaac Newton, which seemed to lead to a network of laboratories.

And then she saw Ben Franklin, a famous Lucian with a long list of important accomplishments in politics, diplomacy, and science. He was also the founder of the Library Company of Philadelphia, a subscription library where members had access to thousands of important books and documents for research. His portrait seemed as likely as any other in the room to lead to an archive.

She pushed open the door. Motion-sensor-controlled lights clicked on as she stepped into a large room lined with rolling racks of files on floor-to-ceiling tracks.

"Well, where do we start?" Nellie wondered.

"I guess we look for O," suggested Sammy. "For Outcast?"

Nellie shut the door behind them with a soft click. They'd need their privacy. They'd just sneaked into the secret Lucian archives and they might be there a while. If they were found by Lucian security, she and Sammy might never be heard from again.

CHAPTER 12

There were so many files stored in the room that the shelves had to be pressed against each other on tracks. There was only room to access one row at a time. A computer terminal by the door controlled the rows to move them around as needed.

Nellie tapped a few keys and the screen showed a prompt to select her language. She chose English, then typed in the letter O.

There was a loud hydraulic hiss and the rows of shelves suddenly swung open like the pages of a book, each massive steel shelf slamming into the one in front of it with a bone-crunching thud as it flipped to the appropriate row. She could only imagine some unfortunate librarian accidentally crushed in between shelves.

When the shelves stopped moving, the screen asked her to engage the safety lock. She clicked YES. A loud snap echoed as a bar dropped to hold the open shelves in place.

She and Sammy stepped forward and began to look through the files. Even though they were in Moscow, the files were in English. The Lucians were an international organization and the Kabras had been their leaders for a long time. Nellie found herself actually grateful for Ian's constant Britishisms, like *lift* for *elevator* and *trousers* for *pants*. The Kabras' unapologetic Englishness was the only thing that made these archives readable for her.

She found a file header that said *Outcasts* and then saw beneath that header three rows of thick folders.

Sammy spoke aloud the thought that had seized Nellie's mind.

"How many people did Grace throw out of the family?"

Nellie's hand stopped moving midway through the files as she saw the letter H. She pulled back the end of a tab to read the full name on the bulging folder: Hartford, Nathaniel.

Grace's husband. The one she'd cast out. The one Beatrice said she'd put a kill order on. Nellie's heartbeat thudded in her ears. This was her chance. She could sneak a peek in this file and know for sure whether or not the terrible rumors were true.

Sammy had squatted down and was rifling through the rows of files at the bottom of the shelf. "I don't even know what we're looking for," he said. "And why haven't they digitized their files, anyway?"

"The Lucians are paranoid," Nellie said. "And you can't hack a room like this remotely. In order to steal information from paper files, you'd have to actually be in here and risk getting caught by Lucian security."

"We know they torture prisoners," Sammy said,

swallowing. "So I'd like not to be in here any longer than necessary." He looked up at her. "What do you have there?"

Nellie hadn't even noticed that she'd pulled the Nathaniel Hartford file from the shelf. It felt heavy in her hands. The cover had a big TOP SECRET stamp across it. She handed it to Sammy.

"Oh," he said, his face inscrutable.

"I just . . ." Nellie started. She didn't know what she wanted with it. Did she want to know the truth about Grace Cahill? Could someone who had cast out so many people from the family have done even worse?

"Well, open it," said Sammy. "We're here. You might as well put your doubts to rest. If Grace ordered her own husband killed, Amy and Dan deserve to know, right? He was their grandfather. And if she didn't, then you can stop wondering. Open it."

Nellie nodded. She flipped open the first page of the file. There was a blurry black-and-white photo of a handsome man in a Burberry raincoat, his head down against a rainy day. The note identified him as Nathaniel Hartford, Ekat. Husband of Grace Cahill. Beside the photo a big red stamp read, simply:

This was the man whom Aunt Beatrice said her sister had married, had quarreled with, and had cast out of the Cahill family against his will. Her own husband. Could Grace really have been so cruel?

Nellie went to turn the page of the file when she heard something, a tapping, like typing on a keyboard. Sammy heard it, too. They froze.

Another keystroke.

Someone was in the room. Someone was typing.

Nellie took a wary step forward toward the end of the row to see who had come in so quietly. Probably just a Lucian archivist.

Another keystroke, and then a loud snap. The bar that locked the row of shelves in place had gone back into the floor.

The safety was disengaged!

Suddenly, the shelves moved, the far shelf crashing into the shelf beside it, and then the shelf beside that.

And where they stood, the shelves began to move together.

Sammy tackled Nellie from behind, knocking her forward from between the rows of files, just as the shelves they'd been between smashed together, sealing row O with a deadly thud. The Nathaniel Hartford file flew from Nellie's hands and slid across the floor.

Nellie whipped her head around and saw that she was safe, and Sammy, too. When she looked forward again, it was to see a shiny black shoe step on the bright red cover of the file. Nellie met the cold blue eyes of Alek Spasky, a steel spike twirling on the end of his fingers.

"Hello again," he said. "Doing some light reading?"

CHAPTER 13

Athens, Greece

The paparazzi were the first to arrive in front of the small stage on the Acropolis in Athens, but they were quickly followed by the Greek news media, local entertainment bloggers, the international press, and a growing gaggle of Jonah Wizard fans.

The Acropolis was a high hill in the center of Athens, one of the most important ancient ruins in the world, a complex filled with temples to ancient Greek gods and heroes. Above the narrow streets of a quiet neighborhood, the complex commanded glorious views of the city and had once been a place of pilgrimage for ancient Athenians. Its soaring columns and iconic monuments were visible from anywhere in Athens, and at its center stood the large square building of the temple to Athena herself, the Parthenon, with wide stone steps ringing a crumbling colonnade.

In the cleared area in front of the Parthenon, Jonah Wizard stepped on stage to hold his press conference.

"Yo, what's up, Athens?" He did a RoboGangsta dance move, which set the crowd roaring. Immediately, the press started shouting questions.

"Who are you wearing?"

"Do you think you have fans in space?"

"Will there be a *RoboGangsta 2*?"

"Yo," Jonah answered. "*RoboGangsta's* a clutch movie and I'm, like, crazy stoked I got to be in it, but my next film is going to be one I'm producing myself."

The fans cheered, the press pressed.

"Is it an action movie like *Quick Exit*?" they wanted to know. "Or a hip-hop musical? Will there be a lycanthrope?"

Jonah glanced around the rest of the Acropolis temple complex. Even in ruins, it took his breath away with its grandeur. As the morning sun rose, the scattered stones and broken columns that poked from the grass gave off a gentle pink hue, and the square temple behind him cast its first shadows on the hill. Every stone seemed to stretch and glow as the morning bloomed.

It seemed insulting to the great artists who built this sacred place for him to be holding such an event in front of it. Oh, how Jonah would have loved to tell his fans about the art and poetry of ancient Athens, the cultural flourishing that created the very place where they now cheered for him!

But no one wanted to hear that stuff from Jonah Wizard.

They wanted to hear his catchphrase from *RoboGangsta*: "Looks like your face needs a remix, skin-bag!"

Down the hill, only a corner of the Olympieion stood. It had once been a great temple to Zeus, but now a mere fifteen colossal columns were all that remained of the original hundred and four. The area around it was roped off, just as the area around the Parthenon where he stood had been roped off, and around four other of the most significant temple ruins in the citadel.

Each roped-off area was the designated launch site for one of the six airships in the Airship X Prize.

Not only would the Acropolis make for striking photographs as the zeppelins took off, it would highlight the lightness of these airships, how they could land anywhere, even among ancient ruins, without damaging a single historic stone.

The silver ovals of the dirigibles floated over the ruins of the temples, held in place by tow lines and attached to metal stairs that led into their passenger gondolas beneath the sleek gas-filled hulls that kept them aloft.

The throngs of visitors and spectators had made it easy for the rest of Jonah's travel companions to slip out of his limo before he pulled up.

"Tell us about your next movie, Jonah!" the press pleaded with him.

"Right," Jonah said. "Check it. It's a story about a mime and the power of the performer to transcend the silence of the modern age." He felt a swell of pride, about to discuss his true artistic spirit in the very spot where ancient Greeks had once worshipped the goddess of wisdom, inspiration, and the arts, Pallas Athena.

Perhaps this moment was the reason he was meant to be caught up in all the Cahill drama, the moment he got to step out of the shadows of Jonah Wizard, Hip-Hop Star, and become Jonah Wizard, Artist.

"So no werewolf?" a reporter asked. "Just mimes?"

Jonah shook his head and the crowd seemed to sag with disappointment. The paparazzi still snapped pictures, but he saw fans glancing around, whispering to one another, and some of the reporters started to wander off. They didn't care about some art film about a mime. They wanted *news.* And they were going to look for it around the other airships!

Jonah felt his phone vibrate twice in his pocket. That was the signal from Ham. He'd gotten on board the Fold N Eat airship safely. Another vibration told him that Ian had boarded the Lucian airship. Two down, three to go. He needed to keep the crowd's attention focused on him.

"Mimes are dope, yo!" Jonah shouted.

They crowd stared blankly at him.

His pocket vibrated three more times. Cara was on board her airship, owned by an eccentric Mexican wrestling billionaire named Guapo Ramirez. A fourth vibration told him that Amy had made it onto her ship, a cooperative project of MIT graduate students, the most experimental of all the entries in the contest.

The only Cahill who hadn't signaled he was safely stowed away was Dan.

Jonah glanced at the ruins of the Erechtheion, a smaller temple on the north side of the Acropolis. The temple itself had been dedicated to Athena and to Poseidon, the mighty sea god, also called the Earth Shaker. It seemed a gross insult to his grandeur that beside the ruins of one of his temples, Dan Cahill was trying to sneak onto an airship sponsored by the unfortunately named energy drink Gas Flight Xtreme.

Jonah saw Dan crouched behind one of the six carved stone maidens that held up the porch of the temple. Two of the airship's crew strolled around the perimeter, looking up at their ship. One of them held a clipboard and studied the hull, while the other looked around. His hands were empty, but on his belt, he had a Taser.

Dan was going to get fried.

Jonah had to win the crowd back, had to get their attention, and had to get the men inspecting Dan's airship looking his way, too. But what could he do?

"We love you, Jonah!" a group of Greek teenagers shouted up at him. He winked at them. That was it! The press might not care about his art, but his fans cared about *him*.

"Yo, check it. I wanna get real with y'all," Jonah said into the mic, lowering his voice like he was about to reveal a secret. Everyone leaned forward. Even the reporters who'd wandered off looked back. "So I've been working on my mime moves," he told the crowd. "And I need your help . . . to, like, get out of this box!"

He started the cheesiest mime routine he could come up with, moving his hands like he was stuck in an invisible box. He pounded on the sides, squished himself down like the box was shrinking around him, turned himself into a squat mini-Jonah, then waddled around the stage on his knees.

It was a performance worthy of a birthday clown, not the greatest hip-hop star and action hero on the planet.

The crowd burst out laughing, cameras snapped.

Jonah Wizard, superstar, was having some kind of mime meltdown.

Jonah threw his arms in the air and broke the silence with, "Yo, why you laughing? I don't want to be a hip-hop movie star anymore! I want to be a mime!"

His fans wept. Some fainted. There were shrieks as their hero shred every last bit of cool he'd ever built. Security had to wade into the crowd to prevent a riot.

That was when Dan bolted for the docking tower of the *Gas Flight Xtreme*, took the steps three at a time, and vanished into the great ship's underbelly. Moments later, Jonah's phone buzzed five times. He was in the middle of climbing on an invisible rope.

Dan was secure and Jonah was humiliated. The paparazzi wanted to know when he'd start performing at birthday parties and bar mitzvahs.

Jonah didn't care. Sometimes saving lives was more important than hip-hop cred.

CHAPTER 14

1,000 feet over Athens (and climbing)

Liftoff!

A loud horn sounded, there was a hiss as the gas expanded in the inflated envelope above the gondola, tether lines released, and suddenly the *Gas Flight Xtreme* began its ascent into the clouds.

Dan couldn't believe his eyes as he crouched beside a storage locker, peering through the bottom of the airship's passenger gondola. The torpedo-shaped tube was held together by metal bands attached to the metal frame of the oval hull up above, but other than those thick strips of what Dan guessed was ultra-lightweight titanium, the entire floor was made of reinforced glass. Anyone standing on the ground below as they took off would be looking up at the bottom of his shoes. He sure hoped the ground crew didn't seem him. He was, after all, a stowaway.

Dan looked down past his sneakers, and his stomach did a somersault as the hills of Athens dropped away, smaller and smaller, until the ancient ruins looked like models on a spectacular train set. Amazingly, he didn't even feel the kind of acceleration that pushed astronauts in movies flat against their seats. He stood up straight, just to see if he could.

This wasn't flying, it was levitating.

There were a few more loud hisses as the giant bladders inside the metal frame of the balloon filled with the gas mixture, causing the ship to become literally lighter than air and to stay that way as the density of the air changed the higher they got. In about ten minutes, they'd burst through the clouds.

Dan bent down again, pressing his face against the floor so he could take it all in. As he watched, the big, round airship of the Fold N Eat corporation popped through the cloud cover below, and not far from it, the oval of the *Galactica Toy Company* drifted into the sky, followed by the wing-shaped MIT airship, which burst up though the clouds, shining silver in the sunlight, rising faster than the others. He knew Amy was on board that one and a lump caught in his throat.

He wasn't up here to admire the view. He was up here to find out if this ship was the Outcast's target or not. If it was, he was ascending to the edge of space on a ticking time bomb. If it wasn't, one of the others was riding a bomb into the sky. Like the Outcast said, "Time flies. And so must you."

But which one of them was due for a fall?

The image from the Internet of the burning hull of the *Hindenburg* smashing into the ground flashed in his mind.

That was the problem with having a brain that

never let go of anything he saw. He couldn't get rid of the horrible stuff.

One of the many digital displays in the corridor showed their altitude: 52,000 feet and climbing. They weren't breaking any world records yet and they weren't even technically at the edge of space, but they were higher than any airplane Dan had ever been on.

Great puffs of white cloud rolled over the oceans and continents below him. As the minutes stretched out, Dan saw the dark blue of the horizon and the long curve of the earth itself. Looking sideways again, he saw the black of space beyond the horizon. He was much higher than the other airships now.

He looked back at the display. 56,000 feet. They were climbing at about 4,000 feet per minute. That seemed really fast to him . . . winningly fast.

Focus on the job at hand, Dan told himself. *The Outcast is going to blow up the winning airship and kill everyone on board. It's up to me to try to stop it. I gotta stop enjoying the view and investigate.*

But how the heck was he supposed to investigate when he knew so little about the actual workings of an airship? Space was cool, but it wasn't like Dan was an engineer.

"It's a waste of brilliant technology," someone said, strolling down the gangway. "All this just so some teenage stuntman can set a world record?"

Dan ducked back behind the storage locker and hoped whoever was coming didn't look down at him. There was nowhere else to hide.

"That's the nature of sponsorship," a woman's voice said. "Someone has to pay for all this technology, and energy drinks are the fastest-growing soft drink segment in the world market. They couldn't resist the publicity."

"But the ship itself won't be breaking any records," the man complained. "Where's the glory for us? All the other airships are actually in this thing to win it!"

"If we hit twenty-five miles above sea level, it will be the highest-ever-recorded skydive and the first time a teenager has broken the speed of sound without the aid of an engine," the woman said. "That will sell far more energy drinks than winning some aeronautics prize."

"I just can't imagine actually jumping from that high up or falling that fast down," the man said. "Who would be crazy enough?"

"You haven't met him?" the woman laughed. "The Flying Falconi! He's a teenage circus performer. They made him a child-size space suit and everything. He got into skydiving to get off his mother's alpaca farm in New Mexico."

"Alpaca?" the man asked.

"Yes," the woman said. "A well-bred alpaca can fetch its breeder over $10,000 at auction and . . ."

Her voice trailed off as the engineers rounded a corner. Dan let out a breath.

So this airship wasn't in the competition to win it. They were in it for a big stunt.

He pulled out his phone to text the others that his

ship probably wasn't going to be the Outcast's target, but of course there'd be no signal this high up.

He hoped nothing went wrong on the other airships. The odds had just gone up that Amy's ship would be the one to fall out of the sky, and if the Outcast decided to detonate early for some reason, Dan wouldn't even know about it until it was too late.

Dan made his way along the corridor, staring down at his feet to the earth below him. He tried jumping but was disappointed that it felt like it always did. Gravity at this height was still ninety percent of what it was on the surface. You didn't get into zero gravity until you were actually in space, but still, he'd hoped this altitude would at least make dunking a basketball a possibility.

Now, that's a great idea for a new extreme sport, subspace basketball. He wondered if he could suggest it to the Gas Flight Xtreme people.

When he reached the corner of the hall, Dan peeked around and saw the main passenger area. It was a round room with the ceiling painted to look like stars. The floor was transparent just like in the hallway, but this was not a space filled with equipment and storage lockers. This was a room for VIPs. There were comfy couches all around the edge of the room, facing out toward the sky so that people could sit and watch the earth below, and in the center of the room, looking like they were floating in open air, a rock band was setting up.

If the Outcast blew up this airship, it wouldn't cripple the spaceflight industry so much as the sugary drink industry.

At the far end there was a door marked NO ENTRY, which Dan figured led to the cockpit. It had a pretty serious-looking keypad lock and a small peephole for the pilots to peer out from. Dan had almost come up with a story he could use to talk his way in and have a look around when the door opened and a woman came out, locking the door behind her.

She was a severe-looking older woman with dark hair pulled up into a bun, held in place by sharp metal pins. Dan recognized her immediately.

Melinda Toth, ruthless Lucian millionaire and close ally of Vikram Kabra and the Outcast.

His blood froze and he felt his chest tighten.

Melinda Toth's eyes scanned the room and Dan ducked back around the corner. Had she seen him?

Dan peeked back around the corner carefully. Melinda Toth was looking right at him. She pulled one of the needle-sharp pins from her hair and held it concealed in her hand, smiling politely at the other guests as she made a beeline for Dan's corner.

Well, change of plans, he thought. This airship was safe, but Dan wasn't safe on it.

CHAPTER 15

80,000 feet over Athens (and climbing)

Dan ran. He raced back the way he'd come, his sneakers squeaking on the glass floor. The hallway curved, and he realized the entire thing was just a big ring that ran around the outside of the gondola, with the main room and the cockpit in the center. If he kept running straight, he'd end up right back where he started, right back with Melinda Toth. For all he knew, she'd turned the other way and was going to cut him off from the front and jab that needle of hers into his neck just for the fun of it.

He needed to get out of this hallway. There were three doors coming up on his right and he grabbed the handle of the first one. Locked. The second one was locked, too. Just as he reached the third, it swung open and a boy just a little bit older than Dan rushed out, knocking him backward into the opposite wall.

"Sorry, pal," the guy said. His face looked pale, his eyes wide with terror, probably not too unlike Dan's face at the moment. The boy had on a T-shirt with his name stitched across the chest. FALCONI.

This was the kid who was about to jump from 135,000 feet up in the sky and break a whole bunch of world records.

"You're—" Dan wasn't sure what to call him. Did he use "the Great" instead of a first name?

He looked right down at Dan on the floor and shook his head. "I'm nobody. I gotta get out of here. This is crazy. 135,000 feet? I'm not doing it. No way. No no no no way. Tell them I quit, okay? Just . . . I quit!"

Without another word, the boy ran away in the opposite direction, his socks slipping on the floor as he disappeared around the bend in the hall. He didn't even offer to help Dan up.

But, Dan noticed, the door he'd come out of was still open.

He heard the *click, click* of Melinda Toth's heels on the floor coming his way and pushed himself up and dove through the door, slamming it shut behind him. He panted and forced himself to slow his breath, to stay calm.

He found himself standing in a narrow locker room. There were three open lockers along one wall and two doors along the other. One door was labeled TOILET. The other said AIRLOCK. There was a folding chair in between them.

The far wall was a window from floor to ceiling that showed the clouds over the curving earth and the void of space beyond.

Dan turned to lock the door he'd come through, but it had no lock. What kind of locker room didn't have a lock? It was right there in the name, LOCKer room.

He considered climbing into one of the lockers to hide, but he'd have no way to escape if Toth found him. He'd be killed, stuffed inside a locker on board an energy drink airship. He had more dignity than that.

Maybe he could hide in the toilet.

Anger flared up in him. He had come too far, faced too many dangers, to hide in a toilet.

He had the sudden urge to step back into that hallway, confront Melinda Toth, and fight. He could overpower her and force her to confess all of the Outcast's plans.

But he had to be practical. He wasn't Hamilton Holt. Dan couldn't knock anyone out with a single blow, and one jab with that needle of hers could kill him. Lucians were famed for their poisons, and you didn't get to be as powerful as Melinda Toth without dropping a few bodies along the way.

Dan grabbed the folding chair and used it to wedge the door closed. He listened carefully.

Click, click. Click, click. She was getting closer. *Click, click.* She passed by the door. *Click, click.*

Dan exhaled with relief, but then, the clicks stopped. Melinda Toth came back. The knob rattled. She pushed the door, but the wedged chair stopped it opening.

"Dan Cahill?" she said.

Dan leaned harder on the door.

"I know you're in there, Dan," she said. "Open up. I promise, I won't hurt you." She paused. "Well, it won't hurt for long."

She shoved again. The door shook, but the chair held. It wouldn't hold forever though.

He glanced back and saw a bright red jumpsuit hanging from a hook in the first locker, a helmet, and a high-tech parachute pack. He looked over at the sign across the room that said AIRLOCK.

He knew what he had to do.

The digital display above the lockers gave their altitude: 90,000 feet, which was about 17 miles above the surface of the earth.

And climbing.

Dan felt his stomach sink to his sneakers. There were only two ways out of this for Dan: in a body bag or in a parachute.

CHAPTER 16

55,000 feet over Athens (and climbing)

On board the Fold N Eat airship, Hamilton Holt felt out of his element. He was dressed to blend into the background as Jonah's bodyguard—dark slacks and a white shirt. He was used to blending into the background behind Jonah, only making himself noticeable when he saw a threat to his cousin, but Jonah was on a different airship and Ham was on his own, several miles above the Mediterranean Sea.

Ham had slipped onto the ship easily enough, but before he knew where he was going, he'd been swept into a crowd of men in suits and women in dresses, and now he stood awkwardly in the center of a round lounge, trying to look like he belonged. The lounge floor was covered in dark blue carpeting but had clear discs of glass cut into it like the holes in Swiss cheese so partiers could glance down at the world below.

One glance through the holes was enough for Hamilton Holt. The earth spinning; the clouds drifting; and the black-and-blue, deep-bruise color of space dizzied him to think about. He didn't like dangers he couldn't lift, run, or punch his way out of. Cold sweat trickled down his spine. His strength wouldn't be much use if the Outcast blew this ship up with him on it.

"Get it together, Holt," he whispered to himself, and tried to ignore the feeling in his stomach like a thousand butterflies fighting a cage match to the death.

A waiter in a tuxedo passed by, serving some kind of meat-stuffed pastry off one of the Fold N Eat trays. Ham didn't want to stand out. He had to look like he was supposed to be at this fancy party, so he grabbed two of the pastries and shoved them into his mouth.

Posters and ads all over the room screamed out the slogan of the corporate sponsor: Fold N Eat: The World's Most Indestructible Airline Snack Tray™ #Unbreakable

He grabbed one more meat pie before the waiter got away. The butterflies calmed down now that they'd been fed.

As Ham chewed, he tried to figure out what he was supposed to do. He wished Ian's instructions had been more specific. How was he supposed to decide if this airship was more likely to go higher than any other, thus making it the Outcast's target? What if that wasn't how the Outcast was choosing his target, or what if he'd targeted all of them?

Ham had no way to know. But, after serving alongside Jonah in country after country, movie premiere after movie premiere, Ham knew how to watch a crowd to look for suspicious activity. He'd spotted the kindly looking grandmother in Paris who was actually trying to steal Jonah's sunglasses to sell on the Internet, and he'd seen the danger in a group of nine-year-olds in Dubai who were being paid by the paparazzi to report every time Jonah went to the bathroom.

So Ham wasn't going to investigate the blimp—er, airship; he was going to investigate the *people* on board to see if any of them looked suspicious.

But first, another one of those delicious pastries.

He grabbed two more and stuffed them into his mouth as he started his security assessment of the passengers. Most of them looked like average business people, junior executives trying not to get caught picking their noses when they thought no one was looking, senior executives not caring if anyone caught them picking their noses, and waiters running to and fro with their indestructible trays serving champagne and appetizers and—what was that? Miniature lamb chops in garlic mint sauce? *Yes, please!*

Ham grabbed one with each hand off the tray as the waiter sailed past.

Just as he finished gnawing the meat off the second chop—and realizing he had no idea what to do with the bones—he caught something from the corner of his eye.

There was a nervous man with a bushy mustache holding a briefcase so tightly it made his knuckles white. He was the only person in the room with a briefcase, and he was the only person not talking to anyone. Ham pivoted slightly toward him to get a better view. The man was skulking close to a locked door that read AUTHORIZED PERSONNEL ONLY in four different languages, and he kept checking his watch. Sweat beaded on the guy's forehead. Ham noticed a slight twitch of the man's eye toward a woman in a navy blue suit.

Ham moved his gaze to the woman as she laughed at some joke a portly Fold N Eat salesman had just made. Without so much as a crack in her smile, she gave the nervous little man a nod across the room. The man made his move, sliding through the marked door and vanishing into the bowels of the ship.

This was it! He must be the saboteur!

The man looked so shaky Ham could probably take him out with both hands tied behind his back. Ham rushed forward, knocking elegantly dressed people from his path, crashing through the party like a battering ram, and burst through the door.

The nervous man with the mustache glanced over his shoulder in surprise and Ham caught him in a few strides, tackling him beside a large catering rack of plastic trays loaded with stuffed mushroom caps ready to be served.

"Oooof!" said the man. "What are you doing?"

"I'm—" That's when Ham realized he had no idea what he was doing. He was supposed to identify the saboteur, not tackle him. If this man was stopping the ship from reaching the Karman Line, they could scratch the ship off their list.

But if he was planting a bomb to blow it up, then Hamilton Holt could end all this and save the day! For once.

He snatched the man's briefcase and held it up as he drove his knee into the man's back.

"What is this?" Ham demanded. "Who do you work for?"

"Fold N Eat!" the man cried out. "I work for Fold N Eat!"

"And what's in this case? Is it a bomb?"

"A bomb?" the man cried out. "Who would bring a bomb onto a ship like this? Are you crazy? I design snack trays!"

"We'll see about that," said Ham. With all his strength, he pried the two sides of the case apart, snapping the lock and pulling the case open.

Inside, he saw neat rows of white squares arranged in two rows, five per row. It reminded him of the bomb from the blimp in Los Angeles.

Plastic explosives.

His heart pounded, but he knew what he had to do.

Ham snatched a Fold N Eat tray from the rack, dumping the mushroom caps on the floor. Then he raised the tray over his head. The man flinched like he was about to be struck, but Ham slammed it into the window beside them with all his might.

A spiderweb of cracks formed. He hit it again and the web grew. The trays really were indestructible. The window not so much.

"What are you doing?" the man shouted from the floor.

"Saving your stupid life!" Ham yelled, and brought the indestructible tray down on the reinforced glass two more times until it shattered.

There was a roar of air, an alarm sounded, and Hamilton Holt threw the briefcase out into the upper atmosphere. Ham felt the whole airship tilt. His ears burst with the pressure change, oxygen masks dropped from the ceiling all along the hallway, and he realized he hadn't quite thought through the consequences of opening a window at 55,000 feet in the air.

"My samples!" the nervous man yelled as the airship began making an emergency descent.

A steel door slammed shut over the shattered viewing window, stopping the rush of air out of the ship, and it began to right itself, the pressure inside returning to normal.

Ham, however, hit the floor headfirst.

Five hulking security guards tackled him and held him pinned in place, just as he'd held the man with the mustache moments earlier.

"Why did you throw my samples out the window?" the man demanded.

"Your . . . samples?" Ham choked out.

"The new Fold N Eat plastic!" The man threw his arms into the air. "I was to unveil the samples at this party! Now they're gone and our ship is damaged!

Who are you, boy? Did Stow N Snack send you? Seat N Eat Industries? Tell me! Who sent you?"

"Who sent me?" Ham was confused.

"Yes! You! An industrial saboteur!" the man cried out. "Keep him in custody until we can turn him over to the authorities," the man ordered the security guards. "We will find out who has taken us out of the competition, and we will make sure they pay through the nose! You do not cross the largest snack tray manufacturer in the world and get away with it!"

"I . . ." Hamilton couldn't speak with the boot on his throat, but as he looked up at the crowd gathering in the hallway to catch a glimpse of the intruder, he saw one familiar face. Toby Griffon—famous architect, Janus leader, and one of the Outcast's allies—stood behind a junior executive from Fold N Eat. He made eye contact with Ham, then smiled.

Thank you, Toby Griffon mouthed silently to Ham, who realized he'd just done the Outcast's sabotage for him. Now he had a boot on his neck, he was under arrest, and his friends were still in danger.

One of them was still on a flying bomb.

CHAPTER 17

70,000 feet over the Athens

Amy was amazed by the students aboard MIT's *Subspace Cooperative Airship*—which they called the *SCA*. The engineers and officers were graduate students, and the rest of the crew looked like undergrads, not much older than she was. From what Amy could tell, the oldest people on board—the professors—were only there as advisors. Even the captain was a PhD candidate who'd trained for her pilot's license. If it weren't for Cahill family intrigue, Amy could be one of these students in a few years. Her curiosity could be a tool for discovery and imagination rather than one for destruction or salvation. She could be . . . *normal.*

The thought didn't thrill her like it used to. Her grandmother hadn't wanted a normal life for herself or for her grandchildren. Grace had *chosen* to thrust Amy and Dan into the family's secrets, and try as she might to be free of them, Amy had to admit there was a rush to it all. Who else her age had explored ancient ruins, dashed through the halls of power, foiled global plots, and now, charged toward the edge of space? Normal was not something Amy aspired to anymore.

Not even a little.

She hid behind a large water filter and watched the students bustle to and fro as the airship lifted off. They shouted numbers to one another, cheering when certain numbers were called out, laughing at obscure physics jokes, and celebrating their success when they hit 70,000 feet above sea level.

"Hold something back until tomorrow, Cap'n," one of the students called out. "We don't want to set the record on the first day!"

"Yeah, let the others underestimate us!" another student called.

The captain seemed to answer with the hiss of the gas mixtures in the balloon above the cabin. Amy saw their altitude on a display screen stop rising. They settled back down to 68,000 feet above sea level.

"All levels are holding," an engineer shouted.

"Roger that," the captain said over a loudspeaker. "We're looking good from up here."

A redhead in an MIT windbreaker and blue jeans stood in the center of the floor and spoke to the crew. "Seriously, guys, you've worked so hard, I think we should all be proud. If you do your jobs, by this time tomorrow, we'll have not only set a world record for subspace travel and won the Airship X Prize—"

Everyone cheered.

"—but we'll have given birth to a new era of efficient, eco-friendly, safe, high-speed transit that could revolutionize the way humanity moves. In the tradition of da Vinci, the Wright Brothers, Einstein, Gates, and Jobs, we are all part of a team that is reimagining the future. All of us! Together!"

The crowd cheered again.

"Except for you!" the redhead said, and pointed straight at Amy's hiding spot. "You can step out now. I've seen you."

Amy felt her blood run cold, but she stepped out sheepishly.

"You don't belong here," the redheaded girl said.

"I'm—I'm just an ob-ob-observer," Amy said.

"And I'm just the crew chief," the redhead said. "I know you aren't supposed to be on board. So why don't you tell us who you are and what you're doing here? We don't appreciate stowaways."

Amy wondered what would happen if she told them the truth. She felt certain these students had a good chance of winning this competition, which would make them the Outcast's likely target, even though they were nowhere near the Karman Line. That was at 327,360 feet above the earth's surface. Blowing up this ship now wouldn't really match the clues that the Outcast had given.

But, Amy wondered, why *was* the Outcast giving them clues, anyway? If he really wanted disasters to happen, he could just tell them nothing. It seemed like he was trying to keep them busy chasing his trail . . . but to what end? That Amy still didn't know.

And she wanted to.

What she needed was more time, and she'd already stood in front of these students without saying anything for long enough.

Sometimes the best way to buy time for a lie was with some piece of the truth.

"I admit, I am a stowaway," she told them. "My name is Amy Cahill and I'm here because . . . well . . . I love exploration, and this was the only chance I could imagine to see something most people my age have never seen before: history being made."

"You think we're making history?" the redhead asked.

Amy nodded. "I do."

"I know Amy," a girl in a matching MIT windbreaker announced. "She's an old family friend."

Amy looked at the girl in the windbreaker, who had the name *Eriele Cienfuegos* stitched onto her jacket. As far as Amy knew, she'd never seen this girl in her life. "My grandparents in Manila knew her grandmother," Eriele said. She gave Amy a wink. "We can trust her."

"You vouch for her?" the redhead asked.

"I do," said Eriele.

The redhead shrugged and ordered everyone back to their posts. "We're going to test the rotational axis thrust," she announced. She looked at Amy and Eriele. "Tell young Ms. Cahill that if she gets nauseated easily, she should probably go to the bathroom now. In about five minutes we'll be spinning at about five g's. Even NASA astronauts puke at that speed."

"Thanks, Katlyn." Eriele smiled sarcastically until the redhead named Katlyn left them alone, then she turned to Amy. "Don't worry, we'll get you strapped in safely before the maneuver."

"Thanks for your help there," Amy said. "But I don't know you. Did your parents really know my grandmother?"

Eriele nodded. "Grace Cahill was an amazing woman," she said, then dropped her voice to a whisper. "Even we Lucians respected her leadership."

"You're a—"

"Yes," Eriele told her. "Don't be nervous. Not everyone is on the Outcast's side."

"But what are you doing on *this* airship?" Amy wondered.

"I could ask you the same question," said Eriele. "In fact, I have to. Should I be worried?"

Amy had to decide if she trusted this Lucian stranger. A Lucian on board a competing airship was *not* a good sign. Could Eriele be setting up the bomb at this very moment, keeping Amy at ease to prevent her from discovering it? Or was she making sure this ship did not reach the Karman Line . . . which meant one of the other ships was the target?

Either this ship was going to explode or it wasn't. The only one who might be able to give her an idea was Eriele. She had to keep the girl talking.

"I think . . ." Amy began, but just then an alarm sounded. "Are we starting the spin?" she asked.

"No," Eriele said, worry etched across her forehead. "That's the emergency landing siren!"

Amy tensed. Was this it? Was this the disaster?

The airship began to drop rapidly. Amy gripped the wall beside her to brace herself.

"All right, team." The captain's voice came over the loudspeaker. "We're making an emergency descent back to Athens. All flights are on lockdown. Apparently, there's been an attack on board one of the ships."

Amy's eyes snapped open.

It wasn't this ship.

"Oh, no!" Amy's heart raced at the thought of Cara and Ian and Hamilton and Jonah, and most horribly, Dan. "Oh no oh no oh no."

"Some joker threw a briefcase out the window of the Fold N Eat and we're all grounded until further notice." The captain laughed over the speaker.

The crew groaned and Amy's adrenaline settled. Her hands stopped shaking. It wasn't the Outcast's disaster underway, it was Hamilton Holt's.

CHAPTER 18

Moscow, Russia

Alek sat on the edge of a large steel desk opposite Nellie and Sammy, whom he'd handcuffed to the chairs he'd pushed them into.

"Did you have a chance to peruse the file?" he asked, gently waving the Nathaniel Hartford in Nellie's direction so the breeze of the file made her hair sway. He moved with the cool grace of a dancer, every gesture deliberate and controlled. "Shall I enlighten you?"

He smiled and opened the pages. He held it up the way elementary school teachers hold up picture books during the read-aloud time.

There were a few more photos of the handsome man shopping for flowers in a Cambodian market, driving a motorcycle through Beijing, and laughing with a younger Grace Cahill on a bench. The younger Grace Cahill looked so much like Amy that Nellie gasped.

"These are surveillance photos," Alek explained. "The KGB was pursuing Nathaniel Hartford as a possible double agent during the Cold War." He turned the page. "Sadly, they determined he was incorruptible."

Nellie thought she detected a touch of admiration in Alek Spasky's voice.

"Ah, now to the good stuff," Alek said as he turned to another page, read quietly to himself, then held up the file for them to see. Across the top of a memo, written in English, ran a big red stamp that said:

TOP SECRET

ANY UNAUTHORIZED READING OR
DISTRIBUTION OF THIS DOCUMENT
BEYOND ITS INTENDED RECIPIENT WILL
BE CONSIDERED AN IRREVOCABLE
BREACH OF TRUST AND RESULT IN
IMMEDIATE EXPULSION FROM
THE CAHILL FAMILY.

"Merely reading this memo could make a person an Outcast," Alek observed. He raised his eyebrows at Nellie and smirked. "I am willing to risk it, I think. You?"

"Why are you showing us this?" Nellie asked. "Is this one of those the-bad-guy-reveals-his-plans-before-he-kills-us moments? Because I should tell you, those sorts of things never end well for the bad guy."

Alek cracked his neck to the left and then the right. He rolled his shoulders back, then stood. The calm of his face had transformed to a red-hot rage. "I am not the bad guy here, Nellie Gomez. You are."

Nellie narrowed her eyes at him.

"If not for the lot of you, my sister, Irina, would still be alive," he told her. His hand shook with anger.

"Irina died a hero!" Nellie told him. "She died saving Amy's and Dan's lives. She'd be disgusted to see what you're doing now."

Alek raised a hand as if to slap her. Nellie braced herself, but he regained his calm and let his hand fall again to his side. He straightened his shirt.

"And yet she is not here," he said. "I had no desire to get involved with the Cahill family. That sort of intrigue never excited me like it did Irina. I worked for the KGB, of course, and did my duty to Mother Russia, but as for the Lucian branch? Pffft." He waved his hand in the air like he was swatting flies. "I never had any interest . . . until the Outcast came to me and offered me a chance to avenge Irina's death."

"So you *are* going to kill us?" Nellie asked. She could feel Sammy shift in his chair beside her. But she had to focus on Alek. The more time he spent talking, the more chance there would be of escape. If he was talking, he wasn't killing them, and the former was definitely preferable to the latter.

Alek flashed her an insincere smile. "Now, if you'll please read this memo, I think all will become clear to you."

He held up the file, and Nellie and Sammy leaned forward in unison to read. As they read, Nellie felt a chill rising up her spine. The more she read, the colder she got.

FROM THE DESK OF
Grace Cahill

ANY UNAUTHORIZED READING OR
DISTRIBUTION OF THIS DOCUMENT
BEYOND ITS INTENDED RECIPIENT WILL
BE CONSIDERED AN IRREVOCABLE
BREACH OF TRUST AND RESULT IN
IMMEDIATE EXPULSION FROM
THE CAHILL FAMILY.

CLASSIFIED

TO: V. Spasky

FR: G. Cahill

RE: N. H.

Vladimir - the time has come and no other option presents
itself. N. H. has become a threat to more than just the
tranquillity of my home. It cannot be avoided any longer.
This is the hardest order I have ever given, but I hereby
authorize and order you to commence Operation Short Good-bye.

So there is no doubt about my intentions, Vladimir, and so
that you understand the responsibility is on me, not on you,
and that I will not hold this against you or young Irina and
Alek, I will write this plainly: I, Grace Cahill, being of
sound mind, accepting full responsibility, and acting with
the authority of my position, order you to execute without
prejudice, my husband, the Outcast named Nathaniel Hartford.
Do it quickly and cleanly, old friend, and we will put this
sorrowful chapter behind us.

Signed and Sealed,

Grace Cahill

Grace Cahill

CLASSIFIED

Alek flipped the page silently. The next page of the file showed an article from a newspaper that described the accidental death of a Mr. Nathaniel Hartford, late husband of Grace Cahill of Attleboro, Massachusetts.

"'Mr. Hartford was said to have died while traveling on a cultural exchange mission in Moscow,'" Alek read. "'Several witnesses reported seeing him slip or perhaps be shoved into the freezing Moscow River. He never surfaced, and though his body was never found, Russian authorities declared him dead, as no one could survive in the icy waters of the Moscow River in February.'"

"Grace—she—" Nellie stammered, shocked.

"She killed her own husband," Alek finished the sentence. "Well, she ordered my father, Vladimir, to do it. And when it came time to help him out, was Grace to be found? Ha! She looked out for herself alone. When my father was sentenced to spend the rest of his life in Lefortovo Prison on charges that he was some kind of gangster hit man, no Cahill came to testify on his behalf. No Lucian strings were pulled. No action was taken at all, and now he rots in prison, while the real criminal died peacefully in her bed and her descendants run free causing mayhem in their wake."

"If Grace Cahill wanted Nathaniel Hartford dead, there had to be a good reason for it," Nellie said. She felt tears welling in her own eyes. She couldn't believe that the woman who had hired her and entrusted her to care for her kiddos had ordered her own husband—their grandfather—assassinated. How could she have been so cruel?

"It is hard when our heroes fall, yes?" said Alek.

He stood and set the file down on the desk. Then he pulled a large suitcase out from behind it and opened the case. Inside, there were two canisters of fluid connected by hoses to an empty third chamber that had a valve with a timer on it.

"It's time the Lucian branch end their foolish and undeserved position of power in my beloved country," he said. "And while most of the leadership is off on Vikram Kabra's ridiculous flight above the clouds, those who are left behind will find a taste of their own medicine most bitter to swallow. Poison always was their favorite." He cleared his throat, pressed a button, and the timer started ticking down from ten minutes. The canisters bubbled as the fluid from each started to mix, hissing and turning to gas that filled the third chamber.

"If you can wriggle free before liquidized acid dissolves this nest of Lucian vipers beneath the glorious State Kremlin Palace," Alek said, "I do hope you'll tell Amy and Dan who their grandmother really was." He moved for the door, then turned back. "Of course, if you don't make it out, I guess Amy and Dan will know what it feels like to lose someone they care about. Either way, a win for the good guy. Me."

With that, he closed the door behind him, leaving Nellie and Sammy handcuffed in a dark office with the red glow of the countdown clock marking the final minutes they had until poison gas flooded the building. The file that condemned one of Nellie's greatest heroes as a cold-blooded killer sat on the desk in front of them.

All in all, this was not one of Nellie Gomez's favorite days.

CHAPTER 19

Athens, Greece

The airships settled at their docking stations around the Acropolis. Amy practically ran down the metal stairs when she saw, on the other side of the ruins, Hamilton being led from the Fold N Eat zeppelin in handcuffs, surrounded by a private security team. Greek police were waiting across the complex with a squad car, its lights flashing. Judging by the pace the men were moving, Amy had about three minutes to talk Ham out of trouble before he fell into state custody.

Jonah, Cara, and Ian were already running toward Ham. Ian looked much the worse for wear, his suit jacket missing and his "fancy pants" torn. She'd have to ask him what happened on board the Lucian airship once they got Hamilton out of the trouble he was in.

Dan's airship wasn't down yet, and Amy didn't see it on her quick glance up at the sky. Right now, though, she had to focus on Ham.

By the time she reached him, the security guards had hauled him halfway across the temple complex and Jonah stood directly in their path, stopping them in front of the great Ionic columns of the Parthenon.

"Yo, that guy's my bodyguard, you can't arrest him!" Jonah objected.

"Perhaps you should do a more thorough background check on your people, *Jonah Wizard*," the leader of the security detail sneered. "This young man is suspected of industrial espionage and perhaps aerial terrorism."

"Terrorism!" Ham cried out. "No, it's not like that . . . I was trying to *stop* something terrible from happening!"

"Gentlemen." Ian smiled calmly. "Certainly, you can understand that my cousin here is not well. He is rather dim-witted. Large, yes, but totally harmless. I'm sure we can reach some sort of arrangement for his release." Ian pulled out his wallet.

"Oh, Ian, no," Cara muttered, pinching his arm as hard as she could.

"Ouch! Cara, would you please let me discuss this with the gentlemen?" Ian snapped at her.

Cara rolled her eyes and pinched him harder.

"Cara, please!"

"Young man, are you attempting to bribe me?" The leader of the security detail scowled at Ian.

"No, sir, he wasn't," Cara said eagerly. "He was just

giving me his, uh, wallet to . . . hold." She snatched the wallet from Ian's hand and put it in her own pocket. Ian's eyes bulged at her as the security guards starting moving again, knocking them out of the way.

"What?" Cara shrugged at Ian. "We couldn't have you going to jail, too! You're supposed to be our leader!"

"I *am* your leader!" Ian snapped.

"Sorry, guys!" Hamilton called back over his shoulder as he was hustled toward the waiting police car. "But you should know, the Fold N Eat checks out! All clear!"

Amy smiled. Ham had done his job. They'd figure out how to get him out of jail once they'd saved the targeted zeppelin. Jonah would probably have to hire an expensive lawyer.

"Hey, Wizard!" Ham shouted back. "If I'm not out of jail by next Friday, could you cancel my date for me? I don't want him thinking I stood him up without a good reason!"

Amy looked to Ian once more, hoping he'd come up with some other way to stop them from arresting Hamilton, who even thought of other people's feelings as he was getting hauled off to jail.

"So Ham rots in a Greek jail waiting for us?" Jonah confronted Ian.

"Don't be daft. He will not *rot* in jail," Ian explained. "He might even enjoy his time there. Modern correctional institutions have wonderful exercise facilities. He can lift weights all day if he chooses."

"You're one cold dude." Jonah shook his head and started to walk toward the Greek police car where Hamilton was being stuffed inside. "I'm going to get Ham out."

Amy ran after Jonah.

"This ain't right," he said as the two made their way back to the group. "Ham's my bro. I can't let him go to jail like that."

"Don't worry," said Amy. "We *will* get him out. But first, we have to save the lives of all these people. It's what Ham would want us to do."

"Ham would want me to make *RoboGangsta 2*," Jonah muttered.

"So you've seen reason?" Ian said as they returned. Jonah nodded but didn't say anything else, so Ian continued. "We have only so far eliminated one of the airships as a possible target, thanks to Hamilton's rather unorthodox methods."

"It's not mine, either," said Cara. "Nothing on that wrestling billionaire's blimp but oil paintings, supermodels, and uninspired engineering. They didn't even make thirty thousand feet."

"Same with mine," Jonah said. "They're more interested in staying low to the ground where all of Athens can see their giant toy ad than they are in actually winning the prize."

"What about Dan's?" Amy asked. "Dan?"

She looked around, but her brother still wasn't back. Just then her phone buzzed. It was a text message from Aunt Beatrice's phone number again.

```
. . . and the expensive delicate ship

that must have seen

Something amazing, a boy falling out of

the sky,

Had somewhere to get to and sailed

calmly on.
```

"Another poem," said Ian.

Below the text, there was an emoji of a clock ticking.

" 'Musée des Beaux Arts,' " Jonah said. "A poem by W. H. Auden. And yeah, it's about that same painting as the other poem, 'The Fall of Icarus.' "

"Where's Dan?" asked Amy. The familiar taste of dread rose in her throat.

They all swiveled their heads to the *Gas Flight Xtreme*'s landing dock by the stately crumbling pillar of the ruined temple of Erechtheion. The dock was still empty. Amy looked down at the text message again.

```
a boy falling out of the sky,
```

"Oh, no, Dan!" cried Amy. She squinted up at the sky, her heart pounding against her rib cage.

The sun was shining over Greece, just at it had been on the day that Icarus fell.

CHAPTER 20

The Stratosphere (134,000 feet over Athens)

Dan stepped back from the door as Melinda Toth began to kick it. He grabbed the red space suit, the helmet, and the pack from the locker and threw them through the door marked AIRLOCK. He stepped in after them and closed the door, turning the latch to lock it, just as Melinda Toth burst into the locker room.

Suddenly, her face filled the tiny porthole window in the door, her breath steaming against it. She was shouting, but Dan couldn't hear a word. He clutched the space suit in his hands.

He couldn't believe it was real. He'd spent hours on the Internet reading about this experimental suit. He'd secretly studied the website of its manufacturer, Orbital Outfitters, to see how they planned to make a space suit so thin and flexible. He'd always cleared his web history afterward. He didn't want anyone knowing how very cool he thought the whole space industry was. Amy was the one who knew stuff. Dan liked being the impulsive one. If she'd known he actually *enjoyed* geeking out on stuff, she might've tried to learn about it, too. Amy sometimes liked *bonding* with him. Somehow, space was cooler when it was just his secret hobby.

The secret was out now, though. And if he ever wanted to see Amy again, he had to hope the suit actually worked the way the website bragged it would.

The material felt too thin to withstand the heat generated by a body in free fall. He knew that space shuttles had big heat shields on them, and meteors tended to burn up on entry to the atmosphere. He couldn't imagine how a boy would survive wearing a flimsy red space suit. The logo on the arm of this suit called it the Secondskin, which was comforting and unsettling at the same time.

It was made out of a high-tech material lined with tiny metal coils that connected to a battery pack. Dan slid it on, zipping it up to the high collar on his neck, then switched on the pack. As soon as he did, the coils tightened around Dan, fitting the suit against his skin with a feeling of even pressure from the tips of his toes all the way to his neck. He looked at Toth on the other side of the window. She gave him a stare that could've cut steel.

Luckily, it couldn't cut through the airlock door.

He was feeling confident. He gave her a wink.

Her face disappeared from the little window. Had she given up? Maybe he wouldn't have to do this after all. Maybe he could just wait out the flight in this safe little room.

Suddenly, a buzzer sounded and the light in the room turned red. A display lit up with their current altitude and below it a timer clock.

The timer was counting down from five minutes.

Five minutes until the airlock opened into space.

Dan glanced at the window in the door. Melinda Toth was back. She grinned, pointed toward the window at the end of the room, the one on the door that opened into the atmosphere, then made a falling motion with her hand.

Four minutes and forty seconds left.

There was another, looser outer jumpsuit to wear. He picked it off the floor and stepped into it, pulling it up over the Secondskin. This one showed the logo of Gas Flight Xtreme on its sleeve and also of the suit's manufacturer, Orbital Outfitters. On top of all this, he set the helmet on his head, which locked in place. Inside, there were digital displays showing altitude, speed, battery power, and direction.

He hoisted the pack onto his back and began hooking the hoses from it up to the suit, strapping them into place exactly as the pictures on the website had shown. He had never been more happy about having a photographic memory.

He caught his reflection in the window at the end of the locker room and he looked the part of an astronaut, at least. He felt, however, like a condemned criminal walking to the gallows.

Melinda Toth stared at him through the window.

She tapped the face of her watch with the glistening tip of her needle.

Three minutes left.

His breathing systems and digital displays inside the helmet were powered up and active.

A quick check of the display on the wall showed the current altitude of the *Gas Flight Xtreme*:

130,000 feet above sea level.

The airship shuddered, nearly knocking him off his feet. The gas mixture was changing to adapt to the thinner air. Dan had to hold on to the wall to keep from falling over until the shuddering stopped and the smooth ride resumed.

When they reached 134,000 feet, they stopped rising.

One minute left.

He pressed a button on his sleeve to activate the auto-deploy on his chute.

He knew how to skydive and he'd read all about subspace skydiving, but reading and doing were very different things. No ever died from reading the wrong way. Jumping from space the wrong way, however, was definitely fatal.

With a loud hissing sound, vents over the door at the far end of the room opened and the room depressurized.

Melinda Toth waved at him through the window as the light on the wall turned from red to green and the outer door on the far wall of the room opened.

Dan's hand fell back to his side. His feet felt numb. The Great Falconi had had years of training and even he was too scared to do this jump. Dan had had a few extreme sports adventures in the Alps, just enough skydiving experience to know that this was a terrible idea.

He doubted himself. He doubted that he could save the Cahill family when he hadn't been able to save even harmless old Aunt Beatrice, and he doubted that he could stop more disasters, doubted that he could jump into the void to escape Melinda Toth.

But his doubt vanished when he stepped to the edge of the airlock.

The sight beyond took Dan's breath away.

There was nothing between him and the orb of the earth below. If he looked up and around he saw only the black of space, speckled with stars. If he looked down, he saw swirling clouds and a vast continent reduced to the size of model on a 3-D map. He could practically see the different layers of the atmosphere stacked on top of one another like layers on a sandwich. He felt tiny against the vastness of space and an almost cozy feeling looking at the earth.

It would've been hard to explain, but taking it all in, his doubts vanished and he felt like he and every other resident of that tiny blue marble drifting below him were on the same team, united in their smallness, all of them neighbors when considered against the size of the universe. He'd never tell anyone, but he felt a surge of what he could only call love for all of humanity. The Outcast was not going to hurt anyone else ever again, not if Dan could help it.

It took a trip to the edge of the world for Dan to realize it, but *this* was his duty as a Cahill. The Cahill family wasn't just a brilliant collection of feuding clans forging history as it suited their whims. The Cahills were meant to be the guardians of civilization, caretakers of the world.

And they'd still get to do cool stuff.

He glanced back at Melinda Toth, whose eyes burned in her gaunt face. He returned her wave and gave her a look that he hoped showed a touch of devil-may-care confidence.

It would've been a lot cooler if his legs weren't shaking uncontrollably with fear.

"Okay, world, get ready," he said to himself. "I'm coming home."

Then he stepped from the airship door and fell into the stratosphere.

CHAPTER 21

The Stratosphere (134,000 feet over Europe and falling)

The first seconds of free fall felt like swimming without water. There was no great rush, no sensation of falling. The air was too thin up at that altitude, and his pressurized Orbital Outfitters space suit protected him from the extreme temperatures. As he fell, he forgot all about Melinda Toth, the Outcast, and the threat of disaster. He forgot all about danger and fear. He forgot all about gravity itself. All he felt was calm.

He moved his arms like he would in a normal sky dive to steer and level his body.

Nothing happened, so he moved his arms again.

After about three seconds, he began to turn, then to turn faster. He realized that steering himself in the thin air this high was like steering a big boat. There wouldn't be an instant reaction to his movements. He'd move and then count to three and the movement's effect would happen. The problem was, he'd already moved a lot to try to steer and now he was feeling the effect.

Suddenly, he was no longer looking at the curve of the earth but at endless space, then the bright flash of the sun almost close enough to touch, then the bottom of the airship above him, then at the earth again, then space, then sun, then the ship, faster and faster. He couldn't feel the movement of air around him, but the dizzying vision told him what he dreaded.

He'd gone into a spin.

He tried to move his body another way but couldn't get any control of himself. There was no resistance in the thin atmosphere. The calm he'd felt moments ago turned to hot panic.

The speed reading inside his helmet told him how fast he was falling. 700 miles per hour, which was 1,026 feet per second, which was rapidly approaching the speed of sound.

It would have been thrilling if he weren't spinning out of control.

He knew from what he'd read about NASA astronaut training that the g forces generated in a high-speed spin make the blood in a person's body flow away from its center through centrifugal force. Unfortunately, that included making the blood flow away from the heart and brain, things Dan figured he kind of needed to stay alive. In a worst-case scenario, spinning out of control at this speed, the blood would get going so fast away from the center of his body that it would need to escape, and the only way out would be through his eyes. That'd certainly kill him, but he wouldn't feel it because he'd probably black out before it happened. The same thing had nearly happened to the previous record holder for the highest free fall, and he'd had years of training before his subspace jump.

Dan felt short of breath. He gasped for air, and even as he breathed, it felt like he couldn't get enough. His chest felt tight, his heartbeat fluttery, and he had no idea which way was up or down anymore.

As he spun and spun, his vision no longer filled with the earth then space then the earth then space. Instead, he was somewhere else entirely, in the living room of their old apartment in Boston, and he was on the Internet and he was watching videos, videos of someone else falling from the sky.

He'd seen videos of the last subspace jumper and now, with every second of that jump clear as daylight in his mind, he mimicked what he remembered.

He pulled his arms back toward his body to stabilize them, groaning with the effort of moving them just a few inches. He struggled to untangle his legs. Sweat erupted on his forehead and his helmet fogged. His vision narrowed to a pinpoint of blue light in the middle of a black circle. He clung to consciousness.

If he passed out now, he was dead. He'd hit the earth as a bloody corpse in a parachute. He had to stay awake to stay alive.

"Stay awake, stay alive, stay awake, stay alive!" he muttered to himself. He imagined Melinda Toth in the airship, smirking as gravity did her dirty work for her.

Dan pulled his arms in, tucked his head, bent his back to shift his center of gravity, and tried to hold that position with all the strength he had left. He ignored his narrowing tunnel vision, ignored his fear of death, and spread his body wide against the air. The lower he fell, the thicker the air became. It was like falling into a pool of cotton. The air against his body slowed him. He regained control, leveled out, and began to fall flat, facedown, in proper skydiving form. The orb of the earth raced up at him.

He felt a wave of hot relief wash over him. His breathing mellowed and his heartbeat slowed. Calm returned. To his surprise, only thirty seconds had passed.

It didn't feel like he was accelerating as he fell. It felt more like he was being held up in the gentle cup of an invisible palm. He pictured his parents, as much as he could remember them, and imagined their hands cupped together, lowering him carefully to the earth.

A chime sounded in his helmet and he realized it wasn't so gentle after all. He'd just hit a speed of 1,142 feet per second, 778 miles per hour, which meant he'd just become the fastest free-faller in history and the youngest person ever to break the speed of sound unaided by any form of engine.

He couldn't help letting out a whoop.

Time seemed to speed up again as the earth grew larger and larger, filling his field of vision. He kept his focus forward, and soon he'd cleared the highest layer of cloud cover and he could make out the shape of the continents below.

He was glad he'd spent so much time studying world maps and satellite images. He knew exactly where he was and exactly where he was going, without anyone having to tell him the plan. He was going to land right in the Parthenon, on top of the tallest hill in Athens.

Once his parachute opened, that is.

He checked his altitude.

10,000 feet. A second later 9,000 feet. Then 8,000.

"Any time now," he said aloud.

Suddenly, his visor display flashed red. AUTO DEPLOY FAIL.

"Of course," he muttered. The parachute's auto deploy wasn't working.

He took a deep breath and squeezed the manual release in his right hand.

Nothing happened.

That's when the thrill wore off and he remembered the Outcast again.

"No!" he yelled. He was not going to be the Outcast's disaster. He felt like throwing up inside his helmet. He suddenly noticed he had to go to the bathroom really badly. He also had a craving for cold pizza. Strange, the thoughts one had before dying.

"No! No! No!" he yelled.

An oddly polite computer voice crackled in his ear: "Please deploy manual emergency chute."

He was at 7,500 feet, then 7,000. Then 6,000. Time had slowed once more.

The emergency chute? Where was that?

"Deploy emergency chute immediately, please," the voice repeated with computer-generated urgency.

He turned his head as slowly as he could. Too fast a move would send him back into a spin. He saw the manual switch on his wrist.

The earth filled his vision, closer and closer to impact. He wanted to jab his arm out and hit the chute, but any sudden moves and he'd spin out of control again.

5,000 feet. 4,500 feet.

He moved his hand slowly across his body, shifting his legs to counter the motion and keep himself level.

4,000 feet. 3,500 feet.

Past the point of no return. He had about two seconds before the chute wouldn't be able to slow him down enough and he'd break every bone in his body on impact.

"Deploy emergency chute now!" The computer voice wasn't being polite anymore.

3,000 feet. He hit the button, closed his eyes.

Still nothing happened. Dan's stomach sank. He thought of Amy, sad that he'd be leaving her all alone when his body was smashed to paste on the ruins of ancient Greece. Then, with a sickening lurch, his stomach rose into his face. For the first time, he felt the speed he was traveling as the chute deployed and he rapidly decelerated.

The drag slowed him, the chute grew and filled, and before he knew it, he was no longer in free fall, he was parachuting over Greece. He was in control. He was flying!

And he felt wonderful!

For about four minutes, he guided his parachute, flying over the deep blue water of the Mediterranean, the white beaches of the Greek Isles, and then the bustling city of Athens below him. He saw the hill of the Parthenon rising to greet him, the cleared plaza where the Gas Flight Xtreme logo had been drawn in chalk on the ground and all the other airships were docked in a circle, creating a perfect landing zone.

He also saw the hordes of photographers and spectators behind roped-off police lines. In just a few seconds, he'd be on the ground and everyone would figure out that he wasn't the Great Falconi.

So he did the only thing he could think to do.

He turned.

He leaned right and steered himself around the plaza, over the reporters, and found himself zooming over the streets and buildings and power lines of Athens. Traffic looked pretty bad down below. Just in front of him, however, he saw a long building with empty bleachers ringing an open track.

It was the Panathenaic Stadium, built in 1896 to host the first modern Olympic Games. It seemed the perfect place to land.

The moment Dan's feet touched the ground and he

ran to a stop, he hit the release on his parachute and waved at the shocked security guards and a group of Chinese tourists.

Then he ran from the stadium and shed his space suit in a hallway.

He couldn't wait to get back to the others and find out what they'd learned.

Maybe he'd brag to his sister a little bit, too. He'd just set a world record, after all, even if the Cahills would be the only ones he could tell about it.

When he hit the street, he did the most natural thing he could think to do after skydiving twenty-five miles from the edge of space.

He hailed a cab.

"Take me to the Parthenon!" he told the driver. "I've got another flight to catch."

CHAPTER 22

Moscow, Russia

The clock ran down and Nellie watched the gas in the device's third chamber expand, a swirling white cloud of death. Six minutes left. She struggled with her hands behind her back, trying to imagine the lock on the cuffs as clearly as possible. Sammy chatted nervously beside her.

"The Outcast is really going to destroy the Lucian base?" Sammy asked. "He'll start a war among the branches."

"The war's been going on for centuries," Nellie countered. "I think he means to finish it. And frankly, I don't want to be caught up as an innocent bystander."

With that, Nellie finished picking the lock of her handcuffs with the small implement she always kept under her watch. Lock picking hadn't been a skill she'd used much in culinary school, but it was mighty handy when looking after Amy and Dan.

"Wow," Sammy marveled at her. "You really are amazing."

"And my soufflés never collapse, either," she said, kneeling down beside him to pick his lock, too.

By the time she'd snapped him free, there were only four minutes left on the clock.

"Can you disarm it?"

Sammy shook his head. "Once that gas is mixed, there's no going back."

"Then we need to get this place evacuated." She looked up at the ceiling and saw a smoke alarm mounted above. She rushed to the desk and opened the top drawer to rummage past pens, pencils, a cell phone charger, and a magnifying glass. There was a stack of official-looking IDs from different governments inside: an inspector's ID from the Russian Department of Fisheries, a parking pass for the Official Delegation of Maldives to the United Nations, and an analyst's ID from Interpol, the international police agency. Lucians liked to go wherever they wanted and it seemed they kept stacks of forged IDs lying around. Nellie shoved the whole stack in her pocket, and below it found what she was actually looking for: a lighter.

She grabbed the Nathaniel Hartford file from the desk and held it in the air. Then she took the lighter to it.

"What are you doing?" Sammy cried. "That's the only proof we have of Grace ordering the hit on her husband."

"And what good is it?" Nellie said as she watched the layers of paper burn to ash, black smoke rising from them.

"Amy and Dan should know about it," Sammy said.

"Why?" Nellie snapped. "How does it help them to know that the grandmother they adored, the grandmother who gave them everything . . . who gave *me* everything, was a ruthless killer? Ruining Grace's reputation in her grandchildren's eyes won't bring us any closer to catching the Outcast, will it?"

Sammy didn't answer. She could see by his face how her anger frightened him.

"I'm sorry," she said. "It's just that . . . this is all so . . ."

The smoke alarm sounded, a loud siren, and then a voice over the loudspeaker in Russian, Spanish, English, and Chinese ordered everyone to evacuate in an orderly fashion.

"Come on!" Nellie said, dropping the burning file in the trash can. Nathaniel Hartford's face seemed almost to wink up at her before it crisped and smoldered. "Three minutes!"

They burst from the door and ran through the mural room right into two Lucian guards.

"Hey! Who are you?" one of the guards demanded. The other reached for his stun gun, but just then they heard a shattering in the office they'd come from, a loud hiss. The second guard stepped past them to investigate. The air smelled suddenly of rotten eggs.

"What the—" he began, but then began to cough, to choke, and a cloud of gas enveloped him. "AHHH!" he screamed, jumping backward. The sleeve of his shirt sizzled, the skin on his arm burst out in blisters.

The other guard rushed forward to help him. "You two stay right there!" he ordered.

"Not a chance!" Nellie shouted as the cloud of gas grew.

The door to the office they'd run out of was bubbling and collapsing. The gas melted metal and plaster along with flesh and bone. The guards were on the other side of it. What kind of monster would set such a device?

"Forget this!" one of the guards yelled. "They're not worth it!" The two of them ran for the exit.

As the cloud grew toward Sammy and Nellie, their eyes began to water. Nellie's throat itched.

The cloud of gaseous acid was coming their way, dissolving the floor as it went.

"We need to go!" She pulled Sammy along down the hallway. A group of Lucians in white coats came running from a lab, heading for a set of emergency stairs. Nellie and Sammy followed.

"Who are you two?" one of the lab technicians asked.

"Just visiting," said Nellie, and she and Sammy raced up the stairs.

"Hey!" another uniformed Lucian guard shouted from behind. "Stop those two! Intruders!"

One of the scientists pulled a syringe from his coat pocket, the skull and crossbones symbol screaming up from its label. "I've got them!"

He lunged at Nellie, but Sammy blocked him, knocking the needle from the scientist's hand and smashing it underfoot. Nellie delivered a swift uppercut to the man's chin and shoved him backward down the stairs, just as the guard fired his stun gun up at them.

It hit the scientist, who grunted and went limp, falling right into the guard and sending them both tumbling back down the stairs. It took all the guard's strength to carry the unconscious scientist up the stairs. Nellie and Sammy took the stairs two at a time, escaping from both the guard and the deadly gas at the same time.

Still, as she heard the sound of the ceiling collapsing behind them, she looked back to make sure they were okay. No one deserved to die like this.

The guard and the scientist were still climbing the stairs, and the scientist was waking up. She was glad they were alive. That didn't mean they'd return the favor if they caught her.

"Run faster!" she urged Sammy.

She and Sammy burst through to daylight outside the high redbrick walls of the Kremlin on a narrow path that ran alongside the Moscow River, from which the city took its name.

Tourists' day cruises and billionaires' yachts motored along the river's chilly surface, oblivious to the secret base turning to a poison death trap below.

The fleeing Lucians were right behind Nellie and Sammy, so they didn't have time to stop to catch their breath. They ran beside the river. Nellie looked back to see scientists in lab coats burst out from another exit barely in front of a white cloud, choking and rolling on the ground, peeling off their sizzling coats.

Part of the historic Kremlin wall sagged, then collapsed as the structure beneath it was reduced to a sizzling puddle of melted metal and stone.

Sirens wailed in the distance.

Two Lucian guards stood from the grass, blistered and gasping for clean air. They pointed to Nellie and Sammy.

"After them!" they yelled. "They did this!"

Sammy grabbed Nellie's hand and pulled her toward the water's edge.

"What are you doing?" she said. "We can't swim it. That water's too cold!"

"I know!" said Sammy. "Jump!"

Just as one of the Lucians drew his stun gun, Sammy and Nellie leaped from the riverbank and hit the deck of a passing tourist boat. Sammy and Nellie panted on their backs. Nellie's heart was racing so fast she wasn't sure how she was still alive. She coughed to clear the tickle in her throat.

A surprised couple in matching neon green parkas stared down at them.

"We didn't want to miss the sights!" Nellie smiled, standing and helping Sammy up. "Ooh, look, honey," she said to him, pointing. "Did we just pass the Kremlin?"

The confused tourists shrugged and let them be.

Sammy and Nellie leaned on the edge of the boat, staring idly at the city passing by.

"I hope everyone else got out of there in time." Sammy sighed.

"Me too," said Nellie. "Not every Lucian is a murderous goon."

"Just most of them?"

Nellie didn't respond. She was still thinking about the file, about Grace Cahill having her own husband killed. She and Amy and Dan had worked so hard to carry on Grace's legacy and to protect her life's work. Had they been unwitting accomplices to a murderer for all these years?

The thought was dizzying. Nellie tried to focus on a clearer question, one that she might be able to actually answer: Why would the Outcast want to destroy this particular Lucian base, of all the bases in the world?

Because it held the archives, she decided. Because they'd been on the right track.

"I think we need to go see Vladimir Spasky," she said.

"In Lefortovo?" Sammy asked. "That's a maximum-security prison. It used to be a KGB torture chamber!"

"He knew Grace's darkest secret. He might know even more," Nellie said. "He might know which Outcast we're looking for."

"Are you sure that's why you want to see him?" Sammy put his hand on her shoulder. "Or do you want him to somehow . . . I don't know . . . explain Grace's order to kill her husband?"

Nellie shrugged.

She wondered what she would tell the kiddos. How could she explain that Grace had had their grandfather killed? How could she explain that Grace, the woman they all idolized, might not have been a good person after all? The worst thing a person could do was disappoint those who believed in her.

As Nellie stared at the river flowing by in front of her, she wondered which was truly colder, the Moscow River or Grace Cahill's heart.

CHAPTER 23

Athens, Greece

Amy stood dumbfounded, staring at the crowd of press that had mobbed the Great Falconi the moment the *Gas Flight Xtreme* docked. Everyone was asking about the teenager who'd missed the landing zone and parachuted to the earth somewhere else in Athens, the teenager who wasn't Falconi.

"Who was this mysterious teen?" a reporter asked.

"I don't know," said the Great Falconi. "But he's got guts!"

"But why didn't *you* jump?" another reporter asked.

"Me?" Falconi said. "I'm almost sixteen now. I'm too old to be reckless."

Reckless, thought Amy. *That's Dan, all right.* Luckily, no one paid the group of teenagers behind the crowd any attention. They didn't even notice Jonah now that they had a more exciting story. The teens were able to stand idly by the Acropolis Museum gift shop as the press went wild.

"So this is what the paparazzi look like from the

other side?" Jonah observed. "I could get used to being a nobody like you guys."

Amy rolled her eyes at him, then her face lit up.

"What are you staring at?" Dan asked, strolling toward his sister. He had his hands in his pockets, and his hair was tousled, his cheeks red. He looked about as calm and confident as Amy had ever seen him.

"How—how *dare* you risk your life like that!" she snapped at him.

"Whoa!" Dan held his hands up in surrender.

"Yo, that was sick, Dan!" Jonah gave him a high five. "They say you broke the speed of sound!"

Amy threw her arms in the air. "When your chute didn't open, my heart almost stopped! You're the only brother I have, and as annoying as you are, I'd like not to see your guts splattered across Europe."

"Don't be so melodramatic, Amy," Dan told her. "There was a backup chute. Besides, you can't yell at me. I just set, like, a hundred different world records."

"Three." Amy held up three fingers. "Longest free fall, highest skydive, and youngest person to break the speed of sound. You only set three world records."

"More than you've set," Dan muttered. "And I had to jump! Melinda Toth was up there, after me. I think she was up there to make sure that ship didn't get close to the Karman Line."

"She saw you?" Amy asked.

"She tried to kill me with some kind of deadly hair-needle thing," said Dan. "But now at least we know that *Gas Flight Xtreme* isn't trying to win this thing.

They only wanted to do the space-diving stunt." Dan caught sight of Ian's torn-up clothes. Ian's hair looked about as disheveled as Dan's did. "Uh, Kabra . . . did you jump from space, too?"

"I had my own challenges on board a dirigible," Ian said.

"What happened?" Cara asked him.

Ian took a deep breath, then clenched his jaw. "I had a brief and unpleasant encounter with my father," he said.

"Your father?" Cara gasped. Amy noticed her hand go to Ian's and squeeze it. "Are you okay?"

Ian looked down at her hand on his own and seemed to momentarily forget how to speak. He stared at the two hands touching for a second, then pulled his hand away and brushed imaginary dirt from his shoulder. "Of course. I am perfectly fine," he said.

"But, uh, Ian?" Amy gestured at his tattered clothes. "What happened to you?"

"Simple," said Ian. "I boarded the airship without incident and made a cursory inspection of the systems. The crew moved with ruthless efficiency, as would be expected, and I was able to avoid detection. I made it to the cockpit, where I listened to a group of senior officers discussing their flight plan and their intention to dominate the competition."

"So the Lucians really do want to win?' Amy asked. "Could they be the target?"

"They *always* want to win," said Ian. "But my father is in league with the Outcast. So no, I do not believe they are the target. I overheard them talking about the student airship. Your airship, Amy. The captain called it their greatest threat. My father assured them that the *SCA* would *not* be a problem. He said he had plans in place to *neutralize* them."

"Neutralize always means *kill* in Lucian-speak," said Dan.

"So now we *know*," said Amy. "We have to warn them."

"We can't simply make an accusation like that," said Ian. "We need proof."

"Did your father say what their plan was?" Cara asked.

Ian shook his head. "Unfortunately, I was discovered at that precise moment by his bodyguards and . . . well . . ."

Ian bit his lip. Cara touched his back, but he shrugged her away. "My father ordered me removed from the ship," he said. "We were not quite yet on the ground when he had me removed. I fell into a hedge."

"A hedge?" Amy wondered.

"Some kind of shrubbery." Ian grunted. He looked away, and Amy could see tears glistening in his eyes. It wasn't only his fancy pants that had been shredded.

Amy realized that the Outcast's poem hadn't been about Dan. It was about Ian, tossed out of an airship by his own father. The Outcast was a step ahead of them the whole way.

"Did your dad say anything else?" Amy wondered. "Anything about what was going on here?"

Ian's jaw clenched. "He called me a profound disappointment, but I don't believe that's relevant to our current predicament."

Amy fought the urge to comfort Ian. He wouldn't want her sympathy and he'd probably say something offensive if she tried to offer it. Still, Ian was basically an orphan himself.

"When I finally got myself untangled from the shrubbery," Ian continued, "I made my way back here. I saw my father get into a town car and leave."

"So he's not on board the Lucian airship anymore?" Amy asked.

"No," said Ian. "There were other Lucian leaders on there, some executives from the board of Omnia Industries, a warlord or two. Top people. I also recognized the captain and some of the crew. They're all mercenaries. The paramilitary goons my father hires for the most unpleasant work, things like clearing villages near oil pipelines in Burma or escorting nuclear waste trains through civilian towns. They're expensive killers and they follow his orders without fail."

"Orders like causing an aerial disaster over Greece?" Cara asked.

Ian nodded.

"He'll probably be reporting back to the Outcast now," said Amy. "Between Jonah's press conference,

Dan's escape from Melinda Toth, and your father seeing you, we won't have much time to stop the disaster. We have to get aboard the MIT airship and prevent them from taking off."

Ian agreed. "All of us won't be able to sneak on without help."

"Yo, I don't think I can pull off another press conference," Jonah said. "The art of mime only goes so far."

"I can get you on board," said Eriele Cienfuegos, stepping from behind a tourist information kiosk.

"Who is this person?" Ian snapped. "Has she been eavesdropping?"

"This is Eriele," said Amy. "She's . . . well . . ."

"Your cousin," Eriele said, sticking her hand out for Ian. "I, like you, am a descendant of Luke Cahill, a proud Lucian, and I am happy to be of service if I may."

Ian shook her hand but remained skeptical.

"You are, after all, the rightful leader of the family, are you not?" Eriele added.

Ian's lips cracked into a smile. "Indeed I am," he said.

"Good." Eriele locked eyes with Ian. "We finally have a leader I can look up to." She seemed then to remember the others were standing there. She glanced at Amy and offered a quick "No offense."

"Oh, none taken," Amy answered with some sarcasm.

"The airships are planning to take off again right away," said Eriele.

"No they aren't." Cara stepped between Eriele and Ian. "The demonstrations don't start again until tomorrow."

Eriele shook her head. "With all the security breaches, the Greek authorities have revoked the permits for the entire Airship Xtreme contest after today. So the organizers have decided to give competing ships one more chance to reach the Karman Line. First one there today wins the prize. And only two ships have decided to participate."

"Let me guess: yours and Omnia Industries?" said Dan.

Eriele nodded.

"We have to stop yours," said Amy. "I'm so sorry."

"The crew won't just stand down without evidence of a real plot," said Eriele. "They'll think any attempt to talk them out of going up was just a dirty trick to keep them from winning."

"Then we'll go on board and stop them," said Ian. "We'll do whatever we have to do to save their lives, even if they don't want us to." He puffed out his chest. "No one else is getting hurt while I'm in charge."

Eriele exhaled dreamily, and everyone but Ian noticed Cara rolling her eyes.

CHAPTER 24

Eriele was able to get them all on board as her guests, except Jonah, who she thought should stay on the ground so as not to distract the students.

"In case there are any Jonah Wizard fans on board," she explained.

"While you're all up there, I'm gonna sic some of my lawyers on Ham's case," he said. "See if I can get him out of jail."

Ian didn't object and Amy knew why. If something went wrong up above, there'd still be at least two loyal Cahills left alive to try to stop the Outcast from causing his next disaster. Amy thought about asking Dan to stay behind, too, but there was no way he'd let her go up without him.

"He has proven himself oddly knowledgeable about subspace engineering," Ian said. "We might have use of him."

"Oh, *might* you?" Dan sneered. Amy thought of Ian as a brother, but her actual brother didn't seem to.

When they climbed the steps to board, Katlyn, the redheaded crew chief, stood at the hatch and objected to the new guests in no uncertain terms.

"We aren't some pleasure cruise!" she said. "No guests."

"They're just kids," Eriele said. "I'll make sure they're gone before takeoff."

"Fine." Katlyn seethed but turned away to take care of more pressing matters of preflight preparation. They were allowed to board.

"I don't like this Eriele girl," Cara whispered to Amy. "She's a *Lucian.* Why is she helping us?"

"Ian's a Lucian and he's *leading* us," said Amy. "You trust him."

"He's different," said Cara. "He's not like the rest of them."

"Maybe you're just a little—?"

"What?" Cara cut Amy off. "Jealous? Were you about to say I'm *jealous? Me?* Like Mr. Brit-fuff-fuff could make me jealous? Ha!"

Amy let it go without comment. She knew from experience that Ian's heart was as confused and impenetrable as the Minotaur's maze. Ian and Cara could work out their relationship issues later, when they weren't at risk of getting blown across the upper atmosphere in the worst aerial disaster of the century.

"Eriele kept me from getting caught before," Amy explained. "I'll trust her until she gives me a reason not to."

Cara cracked her knuckles. "The *moment* she gives me a reason, I'm ready."

Noted, thought Amy. *Best never to cross Cara in*

matters of the heart, Ian's heart, particularly. I hope she knows he and I are just friends.

Once aboard the airship, Dan started to geek out again about the space stuff, pointing at the nest of pipes and conduits that ran along the ceiling, explaining to Amy what they all did.

"So that must be the helium control tubing," he said. "And that's the hydrogen. You see, the rigid aluminum shell above has all these rubber bladders inside. The ship goes up and down based on how much of the different gasses fill each bladder. The engines provide the drive thrust, but it's the gas that gives it the altitude. As the atmosphere gets thinner, the mixture has to change to compensate. It's, like, serious science stuff."

"So where do we look first for a way they might blow this thing up?" Ian wondered.

"The bladder control room," Eriele suggested. "It'd be the most likely place."

Amy looked at Dan, but he didn't make a joke about the "bladder control room." That was perfect Dan Cahill snark material. He must be really into this stuff if he couldn't even muster a bladder control joke.

"Some of the gasses you use are combustible, right?" Dan asked.

"It was hydrogen that caused the *Hindenburg* to explode," Amy said. "If I were going to try to blow one of these things up, I'd aim for the explosive gas."

She looked at Dan again, but he didn't crack so much as a smirk at "explosive gas." He was *really* into the space stuff if the phrase "explosive gas" didn't crack him up.

"Explosive gas," she repeated.

He didn't giggle at all.

It seemed like everything had been turned on its head lately.

Amy was used to being the one providing the information, while Dan rolled his eyes and got distracted. She almost wished there was some historical artifact around that *she* could expound upon. She felt a little out of her element, not in charge and not expert in anything relevant to their mission. She began to wonder if the Outcast was right . . . had she really ever been fit to follow in Grace's footsteps? Was she ever meant to be a leader in the first place?

As they made their way toward the bladder control room, Eriele told Ian about all the possibilities the prize could open up. "Imagine having the sole government contract to put satellites into orbit cheaply and quickly, or to deliver cargo anywhere in the world in under ninety minutes. Or to drop bombs deep into enemy territory with the speed of a ballistic missile."

"Now you're sounding like a Lucian," Cara grumbled.

"One would think an Ekat like yourself would *enjoy* the wonder of engineering that I'm allowing you to see," Eriele replied.

"Oh, thank you for *allowing* me to see it," Cara said.

"Cara, there's no need to be rude," Ian said. "Eriele is trying to be a good host."

"You're on her side?" Cara scoffed. "Figures."

"I am not on *her side*," Ian said. "I am trying to stop the Outcast. We are all on the same side. In fact, if anything, it is she who is on my side, as the leader of the family. In fact, I used to think you were on my side as well."

"So now it's *your* side," Cara said. "You just want my obedience, is it?"

"It would be nice for a change."

"Guys, don't fight," Amy cut in.

"I am not fighting," said Ian. "I am merely trying to do the work I was born to do, while Cara is trying to undermine me by being . . . difficult."

"You think I'm difficult?" Cara crossed her arms. "Fine, perhaps I'll go investigate the system network. I'll be out of your way then. You and your new friend can be alone together without my *difficulty*."

"Fine," said Ian.

"Fine!" said Cara.

Cara reversed course down the corridor and disappeared around a corner. Ian stared after her.

"Just so you know," Dan interjected, "you guys are not alone together. Amy, Eriele, and I are, like, right here."

"Come on," said Eriele. "This way."

Just then three tones sounded over the loudspeaker.

"Three minutes to departure," said Eriele.

"But we haven't found anything yet," said Amy. "If we don't find out what the Outcast's plan is, we can't let this ship take off. It's too risky!"

"It's too late," said Eriele. "There's no way I can get them to cancel. There's a fortune at stake. They won't stop the liftoff without absolute proof."

She opened a door and ushered them inside a small, dark room that smelled powerfully of bleach.

"This isn't a bladder control room," said Dan.

Amy giggled and covered her mouth with her hands, mortified. She was *not* someone who giggled at things like bladders, especially not at times like this.

Dan cocked his head at her. "Real mature," he said.

"This is our custodial supplies closet," Eriele said. "Hide in here. I'll come back for you once we're airborne."

"Airborne," Dan repeated as the door closed and locked from the outside.

Amy, Dan, and Ian stood side by side in the pitch-black closet as they felt the airship shudder and begin to rise.

Amy pulled out her phone and typed a quick text message to Nellie to let her know they were going up.

Her phone dinged almost immediately, but it wasn't Nellie replying. It was Aunt Beatrice's phone again, still being used by the Outcast.

"What's he say?" Dan asked.

" 'What goes up, must come down,' " she read. " 'See you at the Karman Line.' "

They stood quietly for a long time. Amy heard the other two breathing in the dark. The ship was rising up into the atmosphere and she didn't know how they were going to stop it. If they failed, she and her brother and Ian and Cara and all the students on board were going to be vaporized with the world watching on the news. The thought made her want to scream. The closet felt suddenly so small, the walls closing in. All of Amy's old fears of tight space, of heights, of failure, came roaring back. If she opened her mouth, she knew she'd stammer like she used to. She gripped her hands together to keep them from shaking.

Get it together, she told herself. *Now is not the time to panic.* She had to stay calm if she was going to think of a way out of this. She had to stay calm for her brother's sake.

"So now we're locked in a closet on board a flying bomb," Dan said, his voice more annoyed than fearful. "Great leadership, Kabra."

Dan's snark brought Amy back to her senses. If Dan wasn't freaking out, then neither would she. Her hands stopped shaking.

"It's not Ian's fault," she said.

"Don't worry," Ian added. "Eriele will be back to let us out in a moment. She's a Lucian, after all. We can trust her."

"Trust her *because* she's a Lucian?" Dan responded. "I have literally *never* heard that one before."

CHAPTER 25

The Troposphere

Cara stormed off to find the server room, a room that every complex computer network had. She figured it would be in a secure place that would also stay relatively cool, so it would probably be near the outer edge of the gondola. She saw the redhead named Katlyn walk by, and she pressed herself into a corner.

I'm not being fair to Ian, she thought. He never actually *meant* to be a jerk. He was just too oblivious to notice when he was being a jerk. Ian would happily give his life to save any of theirs. He'd almost gotten himself thrown into jail to keep Ham out, and he didn't even seem to *like* Hamilton Holt all that much.

In addition to making big, quick decisions with high stakes for the whole family, he'd had to face his father today. He was under a lot of strain and it probably felt good to meet another Lucian, someone who made him feel like he was a leader, not someone who called him a Brit-fuff-fuff all the time. She decided that she should apologize. Before he could apologize to her. It was a win-win. She'd be the bigger person.

She'd show Ian just how stubborn he was by being the unstubborn one for a change.

That'd teach him. She smiled.

She was about to turn back when she noticed a door ominously marked LIFE SUPPORT SYSTEMS: AUTHORIZED CREW ONLY.

If the Outcast was going to strike, this would be a good place to start. She reached for the door. It was, of course, locked. There was an electronic keypad beside it, so Cara pulled a small spray bottle off the key chain in her pocket and gave two quick spritzes. There were five digits that had more oil residue on them than any others, telltale marks left by people repeatedly hitting those numbers. The problem was that even knowing the five numbers of the access code, she couldn't know the order in which they were pressed, and she didn't have time to try all the combinations. Maybe Eriele knew the code. As much as she hated to, she'd have to go back and ask.

As she made her way down the corridor, she heard the three-minute tone sound. She picked up her pace, trying to get back to the bladder control room. She had to get to the others before this flying death trap took off. If she knew anything about her friends, she knew they wouldn't leave this airship before they'd made sure it was safe, and she wasn't about to get off as long as they were still on board.

When the airship lifted off, she was flat out sprinting through the hallway, not caring who saw her.

"Ian!" she called out, fear setting in. Through a

porthole, the ruins of Athens fell away as the airship lifted up into the sea of white clouds, then passed through them to the endless blue sky. "Ian?" she called again.

A passing crewman looked at her like she was crazy but kept on his way.

And still the airship rose.

Had the others left the ship after all? Was Cara all alone up there? No! Ian wouldn't abandon her like that, would he? He couldn't. He knew she didn't really mean it when she made fun of him . . . right?

She moved quickly down the hall the rest of the way. Dan had told them the Karman Line was sixty-two miles above sea level and that was this airship's goal. 327,360 feet. They had to stop this airship before then, and if it was up to Cara to do it alone, then that's what she would do.

From everything they'd learned about the airship, she had about two hours until they'd reach they Karman Line. Cara wondered if she could sabotage the thing herself to force it to land safely.

The altitude flashed by on a display: 34,000 feet. That was the height most commercial airlines flew. She watched as they rose above it. The sky outside the porthole was darkening. She was beginning to make out the earth's curve, the light turning an inky purple, the sun glowing off the distant clouds. They were rising full speed toward the upper atmosphere.

She recalculated in her head.

Maybe they only had an hour. Maybe less. They

were racing for victory . . . and their doom. She felt a lump in her throat.

She found the bladder control room and tried the door.

It was open, which was a relief. She exhaled slowly, hoping to find Ian and the others on the other side of the door, hoping she wasn't all alone up there. She stepped inside.

"Eriele," she said, seeing the graduate student alone in the tight room, surrounded by levers and dials and keyboards. "I'm sorry I stormed off. It's just that I'm so used to looking out for Ian that I can get a little possessive sometimes." She tried to act casual, not to let the terror in her voice creep out. "By the way, where is he?"

"He is stowed away with the others," said Eriele, tapping at keys on one of the computers. Cara nodded, glad she wasn't alone but also suddenly afraid not just for herself but for her friends. They were all on board now, and if they failed, they were all going to die.

"I am glad you found me first," Eriele said. "You are just the person I wanted to see."

"Great," said Cara. "I think we should just ground this thing ourselves, force it to land before it can explode."

"Excellent idea," said Eriele. "I'm sure that's just what they'll think you did."

"What I did? What are you talking about?" Cara asked, but even as the words came out she saw the

Taser in Eriele's hand, and it was pointed straight at her. Fear had a bitter taste on the back of the tongue, but she didn't taste it for long.

Eriele fired.

Cara jolted as she lost control of every part of her body. Electricity coursed through her, clamping her jaw shut, frying her nerves. She fell, shaking and shuddering, to the floor. It sizzled like a thousand fireworks going off behind her eyelids. She feared her hair had caught on fire but she couldn't lift her arms to put it out. She could feel her vision blurring.

By the time she could see clearly again, she was tied to a chair and the altimeter read 90,000 feet . . . and climbing.

CHAPTER 26

Moscow, Russia

The taxi took Nellie and Sammy only through the first gate of the imposing Lefortovo Prison. The high yellow walls and guard towers told of a place where dangerous criminals were held, not for rehabilitation but for containment. During the Soviet era, it had been a KGB prison where thousands of innocent people were held for days, weeks, or even years, tortured until they confessed to crimes they'd never even dreamed of committing. Many entered those dark gates under the cover of night and never stepped out into the sunshine again.

The current leaders in Moscow now used it to hold their own enemies, mafia contract killers, dangerous dissidents, and cold-blooded criminals of the worst sort. The man Nellie and Sammy were there to see was all of those at once.

After they had cleared the sniffer dogs and the cold stares of the guards, the taxi driver let them out to walk the rest of the way to the main gate. They explained they were there to visit a prisoner and were let in to the public waiting room, where the clock ticked loud enough to echo off the cold institutional tile, and time passed as slowly as the trickle of mysterious sludge dripping from a pipe on the ceiling.

Her phone buzzed.

"A text from Amy," she told Sammy. "They're going up in an airship. They're going to try to stop history from repeating itself."

Sammy noticed her hand shaking and touched her gently. "If anyone can handle it, it's those kids. They'll be okay."

Nellie nodded. She hoped so.

A thick-necked guard stepped into the waiting room and beckoned them into a small office where a jailor in a cheap suit sat behind his desk, peering at Sammy and Nellie through gold-rimmed glasses. His stubby pink fingers tapped their passports. In the quiet of the office they could hear shouts and groans from the cells in the distant recesses of the prison. On the wall, the man had hung a picture of himself on a fishing boat giving a thumbs-up beside the hanging body of a hammerhead shark he'd caught, or was, at least, pretending to have caught.

Nellie looked back at the man, who pursed his lips, clearly waiting to see if she was impressed.

She shrugged. In the distance a prisoner screamed. Sammy flinched, but Nellie keep her gaze squarely fixed on the jailor.

"You are to visit . . ." The man pretended to consult the sign-in form, but Nellie could tell he wasn't really reading. He knew. "Vladimir Antonovich Spasky?"

"*Da*," Nellie told him, meaning "yes." It was one of the few Russian words she knew. The rest of the words she knew were different ways of saying *caviar*, words that she didn't think would come in handy right now.

"Please, do not butcher beautiful Russian language," the man said. "We will speak English."

"Okay," said Nellie, relieved. "We are here to see Mr. Spasky, yes. He's a distant relative of ours."

"Two Americans, family to man like Vladimir Spasky?" the bureaucrat asked. "He is mafia! You know what they call him? The . . . how do you say in English? What surgeon uses for cutting?"

"Scalpel?" suggested Sammy.

"*Da!* Yes!" said the jailor. "The Scalpel! A contract killer for mafia, you understand? And before that, for KGB. In this very building, he tore fingernails from American spies and smiled for their screaming." The man looked Nellie up and down. "He kill more Americans than you have dyed hairs on your head."

"Still," said Nellie, holding her ground, holding his gaze. "We would like to speak to him."

"Impossible," said the man. "He is in secure hospital. I cannot allow visitors."

"But we really *must* speak with him," Nellie said.

"You not speak with one of my prisoners without my permission, young lady!" The man pounded his fist on his desk. "I do not believe you are relative, and I do not believe I have any reason to let you seeing!"

"Perhaps this will convince you," said Sammy, rolling up his sleeve. He showed the jailor a tattoo on his arm: a wheel with Fe^{2+} repeated over and over again all around the outside of it. Nellie wrinkled her eyebrows. Why would Sammy show this man his weird tattoo? Why did Sammy even have this weird tattoo?

"What is that?" the jailor asked.

"You know what it is," Sammy said ominously.

The jailor lowered his voice. "Mafia tattoo?"

Sammy didn't say anything—just rolled his sleeve back down.

The jailor breathed deeply. "You are relative then."

Sammy nodded.

The jailor leaned forward eagerly and dropped his voice to a whisper. "Do you know something about his money? Where is hidden?"

The old saying that in most prisons the guards are prisoners, too, struck Nellie. This one, though, wore a suit and controlled the keys, and was no more than a crook himself. But a crook with power had to be handled delicately, either flattered or frightened.

Nellie didn't feel like flattering, not after he'd insulted her hair, so she decided to put some fear into him.

"Let us speak to Mr. Spasky before we take this matter to your superiors." As she spoke, she reached into her pocket and pulled out one of the forged government ID cards from the stack she'd taken out of the Lucian base, glad that none of them had pictures on them. She slid it across the desk to the man, who scooped it up and glanced down.

"You are from the Russian Department of Fisheries?" The man looked confused.

Nellie tried not to curse. She'd meant to pull out the Interpol ID and pretend to be an international cop, but now it was too late.

Go with it, Gomez, she told herself. Sometimes the only way out of trouble was deeper in. No turning back now. The bigger the lie, the harder it is to disprove.

"Well," she said. "My uncle is Russian . . . and . . . he . . ." She looked to the photo of the man with the shark on the wall. "I'm guessing you did not have a license to poach a hammerhead shark. Did you know that was illegal?"

The man clenched his jaw.

"I'd hate to tell my uncle about it," Nellie continued, bluffing her best bluff. "Imagine if he had to send his investigators to your prison, what would he find other than a photo of illegal fishing?"

The man stared over his shoulder at his shark photo, then turned back to Nellie, deflating like a helium balloon three days after a birthday party.

Ten minutes later, Nellie and Sammy stood in the prison hospital by the bedside of Vladimir Spasky, Alek and Irina Spasky's father. And the man Grace Cahill had ordered to kill her own husband.

CHAPTER 27

"I will give you privacy." The jailor excused himself and cleared all the guards out of the room, closing the door behind them. He cleared the hallway outside the door, too.

"So, uh, Sammy?" Nellie asked. "What's with that tattoo? You were never in the Russian mafia. Unless there's something you aren't telling me about before we met?"

Sammy laughed and rolled up his sleeve again to show her his tattoo. "See that symbol around the wheel? Fe2+? That's the chemical symbol for ferrous iron compound. So my tattoo is a ferrous wheel! Get it? Ferrous wheel? Ferris wheel?" He grinned widely.

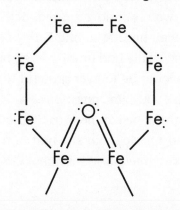

"That is the nerdiest chemistry-joke tattoo I have ever seen," Nellie said.

"You've seen other chemistry-joke tattoos?"

Nellie shook her head.

"Anyway, we're lucky our jailor there didn't have a PhD in chemistry," said Sammy. "And lucky you have an uncle in the Department of Fisheries."

Nellie cleared her throat. "Hey, it worked, didn't it?"

Sammy nodded. "It worked. Here we are."

They stood quietly again, staring at the man in the bed.

The old man lay perfectly still beneath crisp white sheets. He was attached to a heart rate monitor and there was a breathing tube in his nose. His eyes were closed and his skin was waxy. He looked frail and helpless, and she felt sad for him. It was hard to believe this was the man who had raised one of the most brutal killers Nellie ever had the misfortune to meet in her life.

"Mr. Spasky." Nellie spoke quietly to him. "Mr. Spasky, my name is Nellie Gomez. I knew your daughter . . . in a way . . . and admired her, at times . . ." Irina had given her life saving Dan and Amy. It was the only time Nellie had admired her, but for her kiddos, Nellie would be forever grateful to Irina Spasky. "I need to ask you some questions."

"Do you think he can hear us?" asked Sammy.

Nellie had no idea, but she had to try. She had to know. "I have some questions about Grace Cahill."

With that, Vladimir Spasky's eyes shot open and he cried out in Russian *"Ya izvinyayus, Grace! Ya popredaval tebya!"*

Sammy looked at Nellie questioningly. She shook her head. She'd no idea what Vladimir Spasky had just shouted.

The old man tilted his head toward Nellie, reached out, and took her hand in his. His skin was dry and rustled like paper. "Grace . . ." He sighed.

"Do you remember Grace Cahill?" Nellie asked.

The man nodded. "I always try to serve Grace Cahill," he answered in English. He spoke quietly but clearly. His steel blue eyes held Nellie's and filled with tears. He looked sad and she felt a swell of pity for him, until she reminded herself who he was, where he was, and why he was there. "I served Grace Cahill before KGB and after, when I serve the Brava. I still serve her." He'd used the Russian word for *brotherhood*, which was what they called the mafia, which Nellie knew from movies. "I served her always. In this life, I have done terrible things. I lived by the code, the thieves' code, and for my crimes, I will die here, alone in this prison. I know she has sent you to kill me."

Nellie dropped the old man's hand in shock. "Kill you?"

The man nodded. "I have failed her, and this is her way. I am ready. Please, do it quickly."

Nellie's mouth hung open. How could this man

think she, Nellie Gomez, was an assassin sent by Grace Cahill? That was *not* Grace's way.

"I'm not here to . . ." She couldn't even say the words. She'd never been feared before, and to be feared by an assassin just because she'd mentioned Grace Cahill. . . . It felt powerful, but not in a good way, like running down a steep hill and realizing too late you had no way to stop, going faster and faster. All she could think to say was, "Grace wouldn't want to kill you. She wasn't like that."

The man's lips pulled back from his teeth in a gruesome laugh that turned to wheezing breaths. "You make me laugh," he said.

"No," said Nellie. "Grace Cahill was not a murderer."

The old man's eyes met Nellie's again. His brow furrowed. "Grace Cahill lead my family . . ." He paused, then seemed to realize something. "*Our* family, yes?" Nellie nodded. "For many years, Grace led. You do not lead the Cahill family without the stain of blood on your hands."

Nellie felt her own hands shaking. This man confirmed everything that was in that file, the terrible order Grace had given. How, Nellie wondered, would she break the news to Amy and Dan?

"I remember now that Grace is gone." The old man sighed. "I had forgotten. The dead are too many to count now, and I have so few others to speak of. Both my children are dead."

"Both your children are not dead," Nellie told him. "Irina, yes, she passed away, but Alek, he is still alive. . . . We saw him just a few hours ago." She decided to leave out the part where Alek wanted to murder them.

"He is dead to me," the old man said. "When Irina died, I told him my regrets. A life of regrets. And still, he chose to be a killer." The old man reached out to find Nellie's hand again. "I see now that you are no killer. But I have shocked you?"

Nellie nodded.

"Why would you think Grace wanted to kill you?" Sammy asked, for which Nellie was grateful. She wanted to know, too, but she couldn't find the words to speak. All she could picture were Amy's and Dan's faces when she told them that their grandmother was capable of striking fear into an assassin's heart.

"I have killed many people," Vladimir Spasky said. "Too many. And the only merciful thing I have ever done is perhaps the most terrible thing I have ever done. This is why you are here? This is why you have come at last, Nellie Gomez, guardian of Amy and Dan Cahill? Yes, I know who you are. You have come to me as punishment for my sins, which I must confess. I must tell the truth that I could not tell while Grace lived, my horrible crime against the Cahill family. For the one killing I was called to do and did not."

As Sammy and Nellie listened slack-jawed, the old assassin made his last confession.

CHAPTER 28

The Stratosphere

"I think we're airborne," said Amy. "We've been in here for ages. Let's get out of this closet."

"Didn't Ham already do that?" Dan joked.

"Oh, grow up," muttered Amy.

"Dan, open the door," Ian told him.

"I'd love to," said Dan. "But it's locked."

He jiggled the handle. Nothing happened.

He pushed on it with his shoulder.

Still nothing.

Amy heard Dan take a deep breath. He didn't say anything else snarky, and that was a bad sign. Fear was setting in and she could feel her own rising once more. There was no way to know how high they'd gotten, how close they were to the edge of space.

How long do we have? she wondered. How long before there was nothing left of them but vapors in the sky?

Ian jostled his way to the door, squeezing between Amy and Dan. He tried the handle again, as if he had some kind of magic door-handle-turning powers that Dan didn't.

"She'll be back shortly," Ian said, his voice warbling with doubt.

Amy could tell he was losing his confidence as a leader. She was tempted to comfort him, to tell him that it was okay; it was a hard job and he was doing fine, but he really wasn't. They were stuck on an airship rising fast into the stratosphere, and if they didn't figure out how to stop it, they were all going to die.

They waited in silence, in the dark, feeling the shudder of the airship beneath their feet as it rose higher and higher.

Time stretched on.

"We can't wait anymore," said Amy at last. "We have to get out of here."

"I know that!" shouted Ian. "I am open to ideas."

Amy felt around for the doorknob. It was a high-tech latch without a keyhole on their side of the door. There wouldn't be a way to pick the lock even if she had the tools or knew how to pick a lock to begin with. It was a steel door, so no amount of kicking, pushing, or hitting was going to open it.

"We only have one option," said Amy.

"Do it," Ian said.

Amy pounded on the door. "Help!" she shouted. "Let us out! Help!"

A minute passed. She pounded again. She imagined the explosion ripping through the airship and wondered if it would hurt when they all went up in flames. "Help! We're stuck!"

A streak of light filled the room as the door opened slowly. Katlyn, the crew chief, stood in front of Amy with an expression on her face like she had just sucked the juice out of a hundred lemons.

"You," Katlyn said. "Again."

"Sorry," said Amy. "We had no choice. Listen, we're in danger. All of us. Someone has sabotaged this ship and it's going to explode if it reaches the Karman Line. We have to land. Now!"

Katlyn glanced at the display screen in the hallway. Amy followed her gaze and saw their altitude: 115,000 feet above sea level. "We're got less than an hour," said Katlyn. "And I can assure you, there is no bomb on board. The Greek authorities and our own private security went over every inch of this ship with bomb-sniffing dogs before liftoff."

"Uh, *hello*?" said Dan. "We snuck on. Who's to say someone else didn't sneak on, too?"

"Why would someone sneak on board this ship to try to blow it up?" Katlyn wondered. "That's suicide."

"I don't know," said Amy. "But we can prevent it by landing. Right now."

"And give up our only shot at the prize?" Katlyn shook her head. "No. We have worked years for this moment. If we can prove that orbital altitude is possible with an airship, we'll revolutionize energy-efficient travel. We'll change the world."

"If you explode at the edge of space, it won't matter," said Dan. "We'll all be blown into stardust."

"When the *Hindenburg* exploded it ended the era of

the zeppelin," said Amy. "Do you want to be responsible for the same thing happening again?"

Katlyn considered it. She tapped her finger on her lips. "You realize the only suspicious people on board my ship right now are you three. How do I know you aren't trying to sabotage us on behalf of Omnia Industries?"

"That's preposterous!" said Ian. "Would three teenagers locked inside a broom closet really be the sorts of saboteurs my father would send?"

Katlyn's eyes widened at Ian. "Your father?"

"He's . . . well . . ." Ian stammered. He was not helping their case and he knew it.

"Please," said Amy, trying to change the subject back to their imminent fiery deaths at the edge of space. "Just check out the control room. That's all we ask. You can arrest us afterward."

"I suppose I'll have to," said Katlyn. "Come on."

She led them down the hallway toward the bladder control room.

The display on the wall gave their altitude as 121,000 feet.

It was amazing that you could barely feel the acceleration upward even though they were going so fast. Amy wondered if they'd feel it coming down much faster.

The Stratosphere

"Eriele," Cara said. "Why did you tase me? Why am I tied up?"

"Because I need to keep you from interfering," said Eriele.

"*You're* the saboteur?" Cara shook her head. "I should've known."

Eriele nodded. "And I have to thank you for coming aboard. A bitter Ekat with plenty of technological know-how is the perfect scapegoat."

"You're going to pin this on me?" Cara asked. "But why would I sabotage an airship that I'm on?"

Eriele shrugged. "The press will come up with their own reasons."

121,000 feet.

121,500 feet.

122,000 feet.

The higher they got, the faster they rose. The airship hissed constantly now, struggling to adjust the gas mixture as the atmosphere got thinner and thinner. Their speed would also be increasing to help with the lift. Cara squirmed, helpless on board a hurtling blimp of death.

Dirigible, she heard Ian's voice correcting in her head. She gritted her teeth. She had to warn him about this girl before she tased him, too.

Her eyes darted around the room. She needed to stall. She needed to find a way to get that Taser gun away from Eriele. She pulled against the plastic ties on her wrists. They were loosening. As she struggled against her bonds, she also watched Eriele on the computers, trying to memorize everything the girl did so she could undo it the moment she got free.

Eriele noticed Cara's gaze. "Nice try," she said, turning Cara around. "You think I'd let a hacker like you see what I'm doing?"

She returned to the keyboard, but now Cara could only hear the click and clack of typing.

"What have you done with Ian?" Cara demanded.

"Why?" Eriele asked. The typing stopped. "Jealous?"

"I'm not jealous," said Cara. True or not, it didn't matter. She just had to keep Eriele talking. "It's just that I know he could do better than you."

"Oh, like you?" Eriele laughed. "Don't worry. I have no romantic interest in Ian Kabra. He's too much of a wuss for my taste."

"Ian is not a wuss!" Cara said. And she meant it. "He's smart and he's brave and he is kind in spite of himself."

"And that's the problem," said Eriele. "Joining up with the other branches has made him weak. He isn't willing to perform the brutal work that needs to be done to secure the Lucian branch's future. He's no leader. Now, be quiet before I zap you with the Taser again." She tapped a few more keys on a keypad. Cara ground her teeth together.

124,000 feet.

124,200 feet.

The acceleration had slowed.

"Ian Kabra is the best leader the Cahill family has ever had," Cara said, risking Eriele's anger. "He may be a conceited moron sometimes, but he is one of the finest people I know and I'd gladly lay down my life for him."

"You would?" said Ian, suddenly standing in the doorway to the bladder control room.

Cara felt her cheeks blushing red.

Katlyn rushed past Ian into the control room. She stopped short when she saw the Taser. "Eriele? What are you doing?"

"Sorry, Katlyn," Eriele said. "You won't be winning any prizes today."

She hit one more key, and the images on the monitors flickered and turned into gibberish.

Katlyn shook her head. "You can't do this!"

"I already have," she said. Then she grabbed Cara's chair from behind, wheeling her forward like a shield. She pressed the Taser to Cara's neck. "Get out of my way or your girlfriend's going to be in for quite a shock."

"She's not my girlfriend," Ian said automatically.

Eriele scoffed.

"Really," said Ian. "All she does is insult me and undermine me. The only time she has a kind word about me is when I'm not around to hear it. What do I care if you shock her?"

Cara's nostrils flared at Ian, but she understood what he was doing. It was the only way to slow Eriele down.

"She is a sketchy, shady, bullheaded Ekat with as much taste and refinement as a chimpanzee in the zoo, and to think that I would ever call such a girl my 'girlfriend' is quite preposterous."

"You're lying," said Eriele.

"Shock her," said Ian. "See if I care. But I will stop you from sabotaging this ship."

Cara saw Dan glance at the altimeter. 129,000 feet. "Hey, Eriele?" he said. "You know what's funny?"

"What?" Eriele asked.

"You're so busy yelling at Ian," Dan said, "you didn't notice our altitude. Time to change the gas mixture."

Eriele turned to look at the altimeter, but it was too late. There was a hissing in the pipes and the whole airship shuddered. Amy fell into Ian. Katlyn stumbled into the doorframe and Eriele, knocked against a wall, lost her grip on Cara.

Cara head-butted the Taser from Eriele's hand and Amy rushed forward to snatch it from the floor, but it bounced away as the shuddering intensified.

Eriele kicked Amy, who caught her leg and tossed her with a jujitsu throw, but a sudden shudder made her lose balance, too, toppling over onto Cara, whose legs kicked up into Ian's chin as he'd stepped forward to help. They were all on the floor, struggling to get to their feet, all but Dan, who held on tight to the doorframe.

Eriele lunged at him, tackling him into the hallway and jumping back to her feet. She stumbled down the corridor away from them.

"You'll pay for this!" Katlyn called out from the shaking floor.

"Wrong!" Eriele yelled back. "I'll get *paid* for this, and handsomely!"

She vanished around the bending hall, keeping herself upright by leaning on the walls as she ran.

The shuddering stopped when they airship cleared 134,000 feet.

Ian untied Cara from the chair. "Nice job distracting her before the turbulence," she told him. "I'll work on fixing the controls here. You guys go get her. If I can't break through her computer lockout, we'll need her help."

"How will we get her to assist us?" Ian wondered.

"If she's still on board a ship about to explode, she'll help us," Cara countered.

"Right," said Ian.

Amy and Dan hopped up to chase after Eriele. Ian, too, turned but he stalled a moment. "Cara . . . I . . ."

"Just go get her," said Cara. She bent down and picked up the Taser, checked its charge, and then handed it to Ian. "No one calls you a hopeless dingbat but me."

Ian smiled at her. Cara squeezed his hand over the Taser's plastic grip. Then he ran off after Amy and Dan.

Cara turned back to the computers.

Katlyn was already at work. "We're completely locked out of the system," she said. "I can't do anything."

Cara tried. Her first attempt to get around the firewall Eriele had built didn't work. She looked at the altimeter.

135,000 feet. 135,5000 feet. 136,000 feet.

They were still rising, closer and closer to the Karman Line.

There was no way into the system without Eriele's help. Hacking in the old-fashioned way would take hours, time they didn't have. Making Eriele talk was their only hope.

Through the tiny porthole in the hallway, the earth's surface kept shrinking away from them.

137,000 feet.

138,000 feet.

CHAPTER 30

The Thermosphere

They ran and ran, while Eriele ducked and wove ahead of them. Busy engineering students dove out of their way, staring in puzzlement at the strangers racing through their airship.

The corridor forked. Amy and Dan had to decide which passage to take.

"We could split up," Dan suggested.

"Last time we split up you skydived from twenty-five miles high," said Amy.

The display screen on the nearest wall read 200,000 feet. They were 37 miles up now. He had no intention of jumping from that altitude.

They still had 25 miles to go before they hit the Karman Line, though.

Then, *KABOOM*.

Maybe dying in free fall would have been better than exploding.

Dan surprised himself with the thought. Had he really become so used to death he could think about his own so methodically?

"We stick together," said Ian, catching up to them. "We have to think like she would. Let's say you just rigged an airship to explode, one that you were still on. What would you do?"

"Try to get off it," suggested Amy.

"Right," said Ian. "So, Dan, you've done this before. Where's the exit?"

"It's suicide to jump from this altitude," said Dan. "She wouldn't."

"It's suicide to stay on board now that she's sabotaged the ship to blow," said Amy. "So where would she go to try to escape?"

"I don't know," Dan told her. "This is a totally different ship from the one I jumped out of."

"Physics is physics, Dan," Amy told him. "There are only a few places an airlock could be in the design of any airship. I know you memorized the last one you were on."

"Right, fine," said Dan. "I did."

"So use that ship as a blueprint for this," said Amy. "Try to find features that match."

Dan thought. He looked around. The other airship had higher ceilings, wider corridors, and a ballroom. This ship was far more functional, designed for one thing only, to win.

And winning meant they'd all die. Why'd these students have to be so good at designing dirigibles?

Focus, Dan! he told himself. *Focus!*

215,000 feet.

He had to concentrate. Everyone was counting on him.

The designers would want to minimize friction that could slow the airship down. The engineers would want any doors, hatches, or openings to be toward the back to minimize the drag from air resistance.

He closed his eyes, imagined his way through the other airship like it was a blueprint.

"Would you please hurry?" Ian interrupted his thinking. "We are running out of sky."

219,000 feet.

"I'm thinking!" Dan snapped at him. He understood the ship's design now, not just the way it looked but *why* it looked that way. The balloon was shaped like a wing so that it could generate the most lift from its forward motion as well as its upward thrust from the gas. The gondola was a disc so that air would flow smoothly around it. And the point where that air would slide past it would be at the back. Anything jutting out, like a door, for example, would be tucked back there!

His eyes snapped open.

"I know where she's going!" said Dan. "This way!"

He ran ahead and the other two followed. They reached the end of a corridor where a ladder rose into a service compartment above the passenger area, to the highest level of the airship's gondola, just below the balloon's hull.

"I think the exit will be at the back of this compartment," he said.

"You think?" Ian asked.

"I'm sure," said Dan.

Ian nodded.

"Let me go first." Ian held up the Taser. "I'm armed."

"Just" — Amy touched Ian's shoulder — "be careful."

"And remember, Cara needs her alive!" Dan added.

Ian nodded and climbed up the ladder.

Amy grabbed the rungs and stopped before she climbed up. She looked back at her brother. "If this doesn't work," she said, "I want you to know you were the best brother I could have hoped for. Even if you were a pain."

Dan just smiled at her. "Amy," he said, "this is going to work."

She climbed and Dan followed her.

He really hoped he was right. He'd hate for his last words to his big sister to have been a lie.

CHAPTER 31

The compartment had a ceiling so low they all had to crouch, even Dan, Amy noticed. They crept past hoses and pipes and electrical conduits, junction boxes with blinking lights. The innards of the ship.

If someone wanted to do some real damage, this was the place to do it.

Why hadn't Eriele just skipped the whole control room hack and done her damage up here?

"Stupid thing, latch on!" Eriele muttered somewhere in the maze of pipes. Ian held his fingers to his lips, telling Amy and Dan to be quiet. They fanned out, creeping toward the sound of her voice in a wide arc so that if she tried to run, she'd run into one of them.

Eriele was climbing into a jumpsuit just like the one Dan had worn for his dive. It was even branded with the Gas Flight Xtreme logo. She must have stolen it earlier and stashed it away on board this ship once she'd seen it work. The first jumpers had been her guinea pigs . . . *Dan* had been her guinea pig. Amy felt like they'd been played for fools from the very beginning.

Eriele was, however, having trouble getting one of the hoses from the air pack to connect to the controls on her glove.

"Not easy to put on by yourself, is it?" asked Dan. "You learn on the Internet, too?"

Eriele looked up. "Stay back," she warned. Her eyes darted from Dan to Amy, then to Ian. "Let me go."

"Tell Cara how to undo the damage you caused to the computers and you can fly to the moon for all it concerns us," said Ian.

"You should be thanking me," Eriele snarled at him. "I am doing what you're too weak to do yourself."

"You keep saying that," said Ian. "But I do not believe that my reluctance to murder innocent students while the world watches is weakness."

"Murder?" Eriele said as she finally snapped the hose into its socket with a hiss. She reached for her helmet. "What are you talking about?"

"The Outcast's planned disaster," said Ian.

"I don't work for the Outcast," said Eriele. "I work for your father."

"He works for the Outcast," said Ian. "It's all the same. You are in league with my father to blow up this airship. I will not let that happen." He glanced at Amy and Dan. "*We* will not let that happen."

Eriele shook her head. "You idiot. Your father paid me to do what *you* wouldn't do . . . to sabotage this ship so it'd never reach 327,000 feet, so that it can't win the competition."

"The competition?" Ian wrinkled his brow. "This is just about the competition?"

"Of course!" said Eriele. "Where do you think Lucian wealth and power comes from? This technology here, the contracts that will come from winning this competition, they are going to be worth billions!"

"My father was lying to you," said Ian. "Whatever he had you do, it's going to blow up this ship."

"You must really hate him to think that of your own father." Eriele clutched the helmet beneath her arm and stepped to the airlock door behind her. "I told him how to sabotage this ship without hurting anyone and he told me to do it. He had top Lucians on all the other ships, but he trusted me with this one."

"He used you to lure us here," said Ian. "Now, tell us how to undo what you've done."

"All I did was set the gas mixture to get heavier when we hit 326,000 feet. We won't explode. We just won't ascend anymore. That's it."

"If there's no danger, then why are you jumping out?" asked Dan.

"Because I don't want to go to jail, kid!" Eriele said. "That's what the rest of you are for." She smirked at Dan. "Don't worry, you and I will be the only ones to know that I beat your world record. I'm not about to call a press conference."

She opened the door into the airlock compartment.

Ian drew his Taser and pointed it at her.

She met his eyes.

The altimeter read 250,000 feet.

"Don't do it," Dan warned her. "At this height there's not enough air resistance. You'll go into an uncontrolled spin while you're falling way too fast. You won't be able to get out of it and, like, blood will pour out of your eyeballs. You won't survive."

"Unlike you, Dan, I trained for this."

"Listen to my brother, Eriele," said Amy. "He knows about this stuff. He's trying to save you."

"Sorry, kids," Eriele said. "This is where I leave you."

She began to close the airlock door when Ian's hand rose up. A blue bolt shot from the end of the Taser and hit Eriele square in the chest.

She fell back against the hull, hard, twitching and squirming. Her eyes rolled back in her head and the helmet fell from her grasp. Ian kicked it away from her.

"She won't be getting away now," he said.

"Yeah," Amy added. "But she also won't be conscious to help us. We need her."

"She's alive," Ian replied.

"We need her *awake*."

"She said the ship wasn't going to explode," said Ian.

"What if she was wrong?" said Amy. "The Outcast has manipulated everyone to be just where he wants them, moving us around like chess pieces. What if this is how he gets rid of us for good?"

Silence fell. Ian clenched his jaw.

"I made an executive decision," said Ian. "Right or

wrong, I'm the leader and I made the decision that she was telling the truth, that she didn't want to kill anyone. She wanted to get rich."

"But how can you *know* that?" Dan wondered. "You're gambling with our lives!"

"That's what leadership is!" Ian yelled back. "You of everyone should know that!"

Ian had tears in his eyes. Amy saw the weight of responsibility crashing down on him. He was right.

They all stared out of the small porthole at the other end of the airlock into the blackness of space. The lower atmosphere radiated blue below them, like an ocean above the earth.

"If you're wrong, Ian." Amy shook her head, barely able to find the words. "If you're wrong, this is it for us. We're all going to die when we hit 327,000 feet."

She glanced at the altimeter. 265,000 feet and climbing.

"I made a decision," Ian repeated, his jaw set but his face losing its color. Amy knew the feeling all too well. The doubt creeping in. The fear of failure. The fear of putting the people you love in danger.

Leadership was taking its toll on Ian Kabra.

All Amy could wonder was, what would Grace have done in this situation?

"Let's go back to the others," she suggested.

One thing Grace Cahill always counted on was family, even to the end.

Especially at the end.

CHAPTER 32

The Thermosphere

By the time they got back to the control room, the altimeter read 310,000 feet. Katlyn was on a red phone talking frantically to the captain.

"I can't get back into the system to change the gas mixture!" Cara cried out when she saw them. "Make Eriele tell us how!"

"We can't," said Ian.

"Ian turned her off like a light," Dan told them.

Cara cocked her head at him. "That was not very smart."

"She was going to jump," Dan said. "Forty-seven miles up." He made a whistling sound to emphasize the very long fall she had in store. "It was the only way to stop her. No one deserves to be splattered into human gravity goo, not even a ruthless Lucian saboteur like her."

"She said we're not going to explode," Amy told Cara and Katlyn. "Just that we won't reach the Karman Line. We won't win."

"That's it?" said Cara. "She tased me for *that*?"

"Well, winning this contest is worth billions of dollars," Ian said.

"Don't you *dare* defend her, Ian Kabra," Cara told him.

"I didn't mean to—I—" Ian stammered.

Amy shook her head. Those two really had to work out their romantic issues ASAP. If these were the last moments of her life, she didn't want to spend them watching the two of them flirt-argue with each other.

The altimeter read 315,000 feet.

She grabbed her brother's hand.

They stood in silence as the airship rose.

"320,000 feet," Katlyn said. "I think we're gonna make it!"

Amy felt Dan squeeze her hand. Her own palms were clammy with sweat. What if Ian was wrong? What if they were about to explode?

Cara bit her lip and Ian grabbed her hand.

"Do you trust me?" he asked her.

"I trust you," Cara said.

Amy looked at her brother. Dan gave her a smile. His cheeks were pale and his lip quivered but still, he smiled. "You know what, Kabra? Don't ask me why, but I trust you, too."

Ian looked to Amy. His eyes were wide as saucers. His upper lip beaded with panicked sweat. She knew what he wanted to hear. Knew what he needed to hear. She wasn't sure she believed it, but if these were the last words she ever spoke, she couldn't imagine better ones.

"I trust you," she said. "I trust all of you."

Maybe she did believe them after all.

Ian took a deep breath and closed his eyes, still holding Cara's hand. Cara closed her eyes, too. So did Dan.

Amy took a breath and let it out slowly. She braced herself.

325,000 feet.

The moment of truth.

She didn't close her eyes.

326,000 feet.

An alarm sounded. Amy grabbed Dan and hugged him against her. "I love you, Dan," she said.

The gas above them hissed.

And then they started to descend.

325,000 feet.

323,000 feet.

320,000 feet.

319,000 feet and holding, 8,000 feet shy of the Karman Line.

"What do you mean you can't ascend?" Katlyn yelled into the phone. "The gas mixture's too heavy? That's all? FIX IT! FIX IT!"

She listened a moment and then slammed down the phone. She waved her hand at the gibberish on the monitors. "Eriele, if that is even her real name, really messed us up. No way to win now."

"So that's that?" Amy said. "Ian, you were right. We-we're alive!" Relief flooded her as Dan pushed away from her hug, running a hand through his hair and pretending he didn't have a tear in his eye.

"I believe we beat the Outcast at his own crooked game for a second time," Ian gloated. "Not too shabby. Of course, his so-called disaster was just misdirection to keep us distracted from the big cheat my father had planned."

"Misdirection," Amy repeated. Then her blood turned to ice in her veins. "Eriele said your father wanted you on *this* ship, not the Lucian one."

"Yes, and?" Ian said. "My father never much wanted me around him for his victories. He didn't believe I'd earned them."

"But you said your father wasn't actually *on board* the Lucian airship, was he?" Amy continued.

"That's right," said Ian. "He left his hired thugs on board with the older Lucian leaders."

"The same leaders who cut him off after your mother's . . ." She searched for the right word. "Downfall?"

Ian nodded, realization dawning on him.

"Oh, no," he said.

Together, they all rushed to the corridor and found the nearest windows to peer out into the void.

Their altimeter now read 316,000 feet, but beside them, less than 500 feet away, the Lucian airship rose. For a moment it seemed to hang, lit brightly by the sun against the blue marble of the earth. Clouds swirled below. Then its massive aluminum balloon rose and their airship fell into the Lucian airship's shadow. It blocked the light from them for just a moment, looking almost like it was bigger than the sun itself, then it rose higher and higher still. They craned their necks to watch.

It only took another minute before the Lucian ship had ascended far above them, miles above, certainly, they thought, right to the Karman Line, 62 miles above the surface of the earth, the edge of space.

The Lucian airship had won.

Amy saw a blinking light pass far beyond them, a mere glowing speck.

"The International Space Station," Dan observed. "It orbits in space two hundred and five miles up."

For a fraction of a second, the three vehicles appeared in a perfect line and no doubt the astronauts aboard the ISS were looking down even as Dan, Amy, Cara, and Ian were looking up.

And that was when the Lucian airship exploded.

Attleboro, Massachusetts

The Outcast turned on the news as a fire crackled in the grand-library fireplace.

Some overly coiffed foreign correspondent for one of the 24-hour so-called news networks was explaining about the airship competition, then the shot cut away and the camera zoomed up into the sky, where one airship descended to its docking station on the Acropolis. In the distant atmosphere, another burned bright like a brutal star. Bits of flaming shrapnel streaked down to earth at supersonic speeds. Sirens wailed all over Athens. The sky was literally falling on the one-time center of human civilization.

"It's terrible," the news anchor narrated. "Greek citizens of this noble city are seeking shelter. No one knows where the jagged metal will fall. We don't have an accurate count for how many casualties there are on the ground yet, but we are getting reports that there were thirty-six crew and passengers on board, many of them titans of industry and finance! There is no hope that any could survive. This brings to mind the last great airship tragedy, the *Hindenburg*, which, ironically, also resulted in the deaths of thirty-six people."

"Oh, the humanity," the Outcast said to himself, his lips forming the edges of smirk. He shut off the television.

A tone sounded and the painting over the mantel in the grand library slid aside to reveal Vikram Kabra's grim face peering down.

"You've seen the news, Vikram?" the Outcast asked.

"I have," said Vikram Kabra.

"And Alek informs me that the Moscow base has been wiped out as well," he said. "Fewer casualties than you would've liked, but they are sufficiently broken. As promised, you are the last of the Lucian leadership. Congratulations on your triumphant return to power."

"And my son is safe?" Vikram asked.

"Also as promised," said the Outcast. "They were all on the wrong airship. You did well throwing them off the scent, but I do wonder, Kabra, if you really have the stomach to see this plan through to the end. You're far too sentimental."

"I want no harm to come to my only son," Vikram Kabra told the Outcast. "I don't care what happens to the others. I don't think that is being overly sentimental."

"Ian is safe, for now," the Outcast told him. "But know this: If he stands in the way of me getting what I want for the Ekat branch and for myself, I will not hesitate to kill him."

"If it comes down to it," said Vikram. "I will decide what becomes of Ian, just as you will decide what becomes of *your* family."

"As I said" — the Outcast shrugged — "sentimental."

He shut off the screen without saying good-bye, and the painting slid back into place in front of it.

Then he bent down and pulled a thick leather book from the shelf, opening it to reveal the keycard inside.

He inserted the keycard into a safe he'd installed beneath the library floor and heard the soft click of the latch popping open. Inside, he pulled out a small envelope and removed a glass vial from within. He studied it in the firelight.

He imagined the Cahill children running around frantic in the ruins of Athens.

Foolish children. *They think the sky has fallen. But it has not yet even begun to fall.*

Inside his crate, Saladin hissed.

"That's right, kitten," the Outcast crooned, tilting the vial in his hand to bend the firelight through the brown liquid within. "One gram melted amber."

CHAPTER 34

Athens, Greece

By the time their airship touched down again at the loading dock on the Acropolis, the press was swarming, emergency sirens howled, and frantic preservationists were stringing wire mesh over the ruins to protect them from the burning shrapnel crashing to the earth. Amy was awed that there were people in the world who'd risk their own safety to save ancient ruins. She wondered if some of them were distant Cahill relatives. It seemed like the sort of job for a Cahill to do. They were the keepers of history.

Except sometimes they failed.

Like today.

And thirty-six people were dead because of it.

The thought hit Amy like a punch in the throat.

"I think it best if we make ourselves scarce," Ian suggested, tugging at her arm. She nodded, and the group slipped down from the docking tower. They ducked behind an ambulance to hide from the press. Katlyn was already speaking into the camera of one news organization.

"We are horrified by the attack on our fellow competitors," she said. "But we remain prepared to demonstrate the safety and efficiency of airship travel."

"She's single-minded," Cara noted.

"I just can't believe my father did this," Ian said.

"Killed all those people?" Dan asked. "Because that seems just like the Vikram Kabra I remember."

"No," said Ian. "He threw me off the Lucian airship . . . to *save* me."

Amy saw him struggling with the thought that he owed his life to the same murderer who'd blown up the airship, the same murderer who'd plotted against him and disowned him, and betrayed him over and over again.

Amy looked over at Cara, who had rested her hand on Ian's back. There was a time Amy thought that Ian had a crush on her. He'd blown that in spectacular fashion, being about as conceited and duplicitous as any Kabra could be. She hoped Ian wouldn't blow it the same way with Cara Pierce. Amy had really come to like that girl. She was glad Ian had a friend to help get through the grief that was sure to come. He was still the leader of the family and on his watch thirty-six people had just been killed. They were bloodthirsty Lucians, but their deaths were still a tragedy.

"Yo, Kabra." Jonah appeared around the back of the ambulance. "I got a car waiting, Ham's driving, and we better jet before the Greek cops starts asking questions."

"Ham?" Amy asked. "He's out?"

"In more ways than one," Dan said, but no one felt much like laughing at the moment.

"My lawyers earn more than theirs do," Jonah said. "Plus, I made a donation to the mayor's reelection fund."

"A Janus thinking like a Lucian," Ian marveled. "The world really has turned on its head."

"Guess so," said Jonah.

"Okay, everyone," Ian commanded. "Let's follow Jonah."

Amy and the others, of course, already had, and Ian had to jog to catch up.

The moment they climbed into the big black sedan, Hamilton eased the car from the parking lot with an authoritative wave at the security guards, as if it was perfectly natural for a van of kids to be driving away in the middle of an aerial disaster.

Amy stared out the window, lost in her own thoughts.

Ian's father and the Outcast had distracted them on purpose, put them on the wrong airship to keep them occupied while he worked his cruel plan elsewhere. They'd been running around trying to stop him, and it had all been pointless.

She wondered what the Outcast's endgame was. He'd taken out the Lucian leadership, who were already on his side, killed countless innocent people, and destroyed a potentially profitable industry . . . and for what? What did he *gain*?

So far, his only gain seemed to be keeping Amy, Dan, Ian, Cara, Jonah, and Ham busy trying to stop him.

And now they'd failed.

Her phone buzzed in her pocket and she pulled it out. There was a text from Aunt Beatrice's number.

Tie Game

Amy's face turned red. She pressed the call-back button.

She braced herself as the phone rang.

She was tired of feeling helpless. She was tired of chasing disasters. She wanted to chase the *cause* of the disasters. She wanted to bring the fight to him and bring him to justice for Aunt Beatrice and for all those people on the airship he'd destroyed.

It wasn't a pretty feeling, but Amy didn't only want justice. She wanted revenge.

Her call went to voice mail.

"Listen to me, whoever you are," Amy said coldly into the phone. "You are not fit to lead the Cahill family and I promise you this: We will find you, we will stop you, and we will win. You hear me?" She knew she was yelling now. She couldn't help it. "You can't treat us like pawns in your game anymore! We will *end* you, you monster! You hear me? We. Will. End. You!"

She hung up the phone.

The others were staring at her.

"Sorry," she said. "I just wanted him to know we weren't backing down."

One look at Ian told Amy that they were on the same page. His face was filled with that cold Kabra fury she knew all too well.

"Intense," Dan said. "But you're right." He looked up at the sky through which he'd so recently flown. "We have to stop him. Whatever it takes."

"And we will," said Ian.

They were Cahills, one and all, and they did *not* do failure. They would not be victims. They would not let the Outcast defeat them.

Amy's phone buzzed in her hand once more. For a moment, she feared it was the Outcast calling back to gloat, but her heart lifted like an airship when she saw it was Nellie calling.

"Oh, Nellie, did you see what happened?" Amy's voice cracked.

"I saw, kiddo," Nellie said. "And I'm so sorry, but I'm glad to hear your voice. Are you guys all okay?"

"We're all safe," said Amy. "But we're pretty far from okay."

"Are you sitting down?" Nellie asked.

"Yeah," said Amy. "We're in the car."

"Listen, I hate to make things worse for you right now," said Nellie. "But I have some news."

"What is it?" Amy asked. She didn't like the quaver in Nellie's voice.

"First off," Nellie said, "the Outcast destroyed the Lucian base in Moscow. I don't know how many people he killed, but—but it was brutal, Amy. Gruesome. He used an acid bomb."

Nellie was not someone easily rattled, but she sounded shaken up.

"He's wiping out the other branches," Amy said, suddenly aware of a part of the Outcast's plan that had been invisible before. This was the misdirection, perhaps. All this death and destruction just to keep them busy so he could attack the Lucian branch?

"There's more," Nellie continue. "Brace yourself, kiddos. Grace wasn't exactly the woman we thought she was."

"What do you mean?" Amy asked. She felt her chest tightening, a terrible sense of foreboding.

"Just wait," Nellie said. "Please remember, Amy, that you are your *own* person. You're not your mother, or your father, and you're not your grandmother Grace. You are Amy Cahill and you are one of the most amazing people I have ever known. I don't want you to forget that."

"Okay . . ." said Amy, biting her lip now. "Nellie, you're worrying me."

"I think you need to be worried, kiddo," Nellie said. "Because Grace's husband . . . your grandfather . . . well . . ." She heard Nellie swallow loudly, then take a deep breath. "Your grandfather is alive. And he's got a very good reason to want revenge."